Summat Else

ROYSTON TESTER

SUMMAT ELSE

The Porcupine's Quill

Library and Archives Canada Cataloguing in Publication

Tester, Royston Mark
Summat else / Royston Tester.

Short stories.
ISBN 0-88984-257-4

I. Title.

PS8639.E88S84 2004   C813'.6   C2004-904987-9

1   2   3   4   ·   06   05   04

Published by The Porcupine's Quill,
68 Main Street, Erin, Ontario NOB 1TO.
www.sentex.net/~pql

Readied for the press by John Metcalf; copy edited by Doris Cowan.

Represented in Canada by the Literary Press Group.
Trade orders are available from University of Toronto Press.

We acknowledge the support of the Ontario Arts Council,
and the Canada Council for the Arts for our publishing program.
The financial support of the Government of Canada
through the Book Publishing Industry Development Program
is also gratefully acknowledged. Thanks, also, to the Government of Ontario
through the Ontario Media Development Corporation's
Ontario Book Initiative.

For Anna Omedes Regàs

Table of Contents

One has not great hopes from Birmingham. I always say there is something direful in the sound.

– Jane Austen, *Emma*

PART ONE

NOW SHOWING

'Treasure Trove!' said a ruddy-faced man on the doorstep, though it seemed to cost him some effort. 'We spoke on the telephone.'

Irish.

'Mr O'Dowd,' I replied, recognizing his sketch from the Yellow Pages.

The hallway was a squeeze, but he seemed familiar enough with bottleneck canyons. Mr O'Dowd planted a cigarette fairly and squarely between his lips, lit it, and set about a routine. I left him to tramp the rooms upstairs and down. It was comforting to hear someone else walking the boards.

The post was lying on the floor, most conspicuously a tubular package from Brevitt and Sons Funeral Home.

I froze.

More of Vera's fragments?

Apprehensively, I sliced it open.

Not to worry. Melissa Braithwaite had sent a copy of the *Birmingham Evening Mail* – the front-page headline a regrettable 'POL POT FEARED DEAD' – so that I would have a record of Ma's death announcement in the classifieds on page seventy-eight.

The tiniest column indicated a funeral service in St. John the Baptist at 10:45 a.m., followed by cremation at Lodge Hill at 11. Strange, I thought. It would take at least twenty minutes to drive from the church in Longbridge to the crematorium in Selly Oak – loading and unloading. Services were shorter these days, I guessed. But how did they manage a schedule like that? Was it a misprint? Did I care?

Strangely I did. I cared that someone had dispatched Ma properly.

Grief working on my soul at last.

Where was the time to carry out Vera's wishes – so clearly

spelled out on her prepaid funeral form – to sing 'Abide with Me' and 'Jesu, Lover of My Soul' return her to the hearse, drive to Lodge Hill cemetery, say prayers, cremate the body and then scatter ashes over a Garden of Remembrance? An hour or more, surely.

'These clothes for me?' yelled Mr O'Dowd from the front bedroom.

'Women's shelter.'

'Pity, because … fur stole … goodness ….'

His grim voice trailed off like rosary mumbo.

He appeared on the landing as though he'd seen a ghost but was trying desperately to be upbeat about that as well. Maybe he had seen her. Vera was part of the floral wallpaper, not just ashes open in an urn on the hall window sill (I'd misplaced the lid). Or maybe it was a shock that Vera's fur – like the rest of her expensive-looking wardrobe – was fake, steadfastly synthetic.

'Long way from home then, are you?' he said.

In an elbow-patched jacket, Mr O'Dowd was every bit the farmer, an impression deepened by his muddied – or dunged – wellington boots. And that his card indicated a dairy business as well as 'collectibles'.

'In a manner of speaking. Where are you from?'

He lumbered down the stairs, cigarette ash tumbling on his notes.

'Out Kidderminster way. Never forget your roots though, do you?' he said, sighing with the weightiness of reflection.

'Never.'

Well over fifty, Mr O'Dowd hooked a strand of longish hair over his ear and tapped his belly. He was trying to be jaunty – but with such a tragic expression – that I began to sense something chronically wrong.

'We all come from somewhere,' he added.

Platitudes-while-you-work. Maybe this was how he cheered himself up. Puss in Boots – the man was not really interested in *conversation*.

'Don't we,' I replied, sellotaping a pack of dominoes.

Mr O'Dowd dragged feverishly on the cigarette, jotting one thing after another on his clipboard. A nostril-nipping odour of manure – or putrefaction – rising with the trail of nicotine. Livestock? I couldn't make it out.

'Marked sofa, stereo functional. Hm, hm,' he went on, smoke billowing from his nostrils. 'First-rate job of organizing, Mr Jones, I might say. Makes *my* chore a lot easier.'

I nodded.

He gave off the kind of authority one immediately finds suspect. The drinker's marshmallow nose made him seem precarious. A secret, devastating life behind closed doors, perhaps. Or was it the desultory chatter-patter as he sifted and shuffled the detritus in his midst?

'My condolences, by the way,' he said, peering at the underside of a serving dish. 'Mrs Jones was one of a kind, so I heard. Adored by everyone hereabouts.'

'Saint,' I replied. Such was the popular – and misguided – fancy.

'Was she getting old?' he enquired, stirring about in a box containing the many – and highly ornamented – clocks that graced Vera's universe.

'Eighty-two.'

'Ah, well.'

He held up one of the more spectacular clocks, a petite face in a bonnet of golden plastic sunburst. Bow-tied at the chin in glitter.

'Remarkable,' he said. 'Just needs a battery.'

'Her heart gave out,' I told him.

Though he must have spent a good deal of time in Birmingham, clearing the vestiges of poverty from deceased pensioners' council houses, I noticed he couldn't hide disappointment at the inventory of number 3 Edenhurst.

'Wonky tickers,' he replied. 'Most of them go that way.'

I wished I had something more remarkable to sell him, raise his dampened spirits. But surely he didn't expect a windfall from the Joneses' house. This was Longbridge Lane, not Solihull.

'She ran on a pig's valve,' I told him. 'Had it fitted years ago.'

'That so? Pig, hm?'

'She always said it'd outlive her.'

'Saved her bacon though eh, Mr Jones?'

'Right.'

The clocks weren't just garish. Mr O'Dowd didn't know how much I wanted to trample their imperturbable faces, hurl them against windows for the unlived hours they'd counted. It was I who should have opened up. Not Vera. Or Mr O'Dowd.

'More clocks than the Swiss,' I explained.

Together we gazed at these ugly, planetary faces. He nodded sadly at the numerals. I felt like I'd brought down the sky itself from Vera's home and crammed it into banana boxes.

Mr O'Dowd snapped out of distraction – as did I – and moved away.

The man's bringing me to rock bottom, I thought, as we went in and out of rooms like chill air. He was better left alone. I needed respite.

Ring Melissa Braithwaite, why don't you? There must have been a funeral somewhere in the split second allotted by Brevitt and Sons. I had to find out how they managed it.

'I know, sir,' Melissa said, at the funeral end, 'it does seem a bit rushed, doesn't it? But Lodge Hill is a hectic place after the winter months.'

'How about at St. John's – the church service? Two hymns, prayers, plus the drive. In fifteen minutes?'

'Yes, Mr Jones. Probably less than that.'

'Less?'

'"Abide with Me" as the casket goes down the aisle. They only sing one verse, two at most. Short prayer from the vicar and a few words. Congregation says "Amen." "Jesu, Lover of my Soul" on the way back out. The casket doesn't have to stay until singing finishes. Anyway, it's only a verse or two. Down Longbridge Lane to the Bristol Road in our hearse. Traffic's very light of a weekday morning. Brevitt's drivers know all the speed traps; put their foot down when they need to.'

'Crafty,' I said, imagining Melissa's *frisson*. How did St. John's geriatrics keep up? With artificial hips and walking sticks, titanium knee joints and wobbly walkers. Most of them travelled by bus, if they spotted one.

'The crematorium operates on a "first-come" basis. But weekday *mornings* are slow. Your mother's lucky day! No waiting in a queue, most like. Coffin goes down the chapel and onto a platform. Mourners at the side entrance. Short prayer....'

'Congregation says "Amen"?'

'Exactly. It sounds a hurry. But done with the greatest of respect, Mr Jones. I know it would have been a lovely funeral. Your mother so insisted on the Basic Package.'

'It cost over a thousand pounds.'

Melissa was adept at *the pause*.

'Melissa?'

'The actual cremation takes place *after* the congregation has left,' she sailed on. 'Exit right, that is. The ashes stowed as requested. All tags are removed from bouquets laid down outside on the grass and are given to family – I believe you received yours – so that thank-you notes may be posted to the senders.'

Melissa was *reading* to me.

I felt giddy.

The whole drama sounded like fast-forward Lego. How could you honour someone's life ushered in and out like that?

But then again, I had not even shown up in England. Remained at my post at Toronto's Union Station – 'Lost and Found' attendant for rail commuters.

Ma and I had *history*.

'Lots of people are involved, Mr Jones. Before and after the actual funeral. It's a pity you couldn't view the body here in our Sanctuary of Rest, for instance. A lot of people viewed. Your mother looked very peaceful.'

'Yes, I'm sure.'

'It was everything she wanted, Mr Jones.'

'It was.'

'One little thing before we hang up the telephone, sir.'

I want the money back, Melissa. 'Yes?'

'The urn, Mr Jones.'

'It's here. Open on my window sill for all to see.'

'Lovely,' purred Melissa. 'We included our statement with the Birmingham newspaper.'

'Statement?'

'Our account, sir. For the urn.'

'I guess it's not part of the Basic?'

'Oh, no.'

I left *her* a pause.

'Can I be of any more assistance then, Mr Jones?' she said, compassionately. No challenging *this* young miss.

'Hardly,' I replied, failing to sound as gracious and charming as Melissa Braithwaite.

'Our condolences once again, Mr Jones,' she added.

'Just don't bill me for them,' I said, putting down the link to Breakneck Cremation.

Now I knew.

Vera *had* anticipated the farce of her remaining minutes on earth. I guarantee she was feeling less than peaceful in their Sanctuary of Rest at Brevitt and Sons. Stretched out and *viewed* in the Basic Package. The old warhorse was bracing herself for next day's disposal. A smirk on that painted face.

Brevitt's runs on piecework. The *Sons* must be on permanent holiday with that kind of income per mummy. What a lucrative market. The English Midlands was crawling with the near dead.

But before I could worry any more about Vera's funfair funeral or a replacement urn lid, the O'Dowd wandered past – like Hamlet's ghost – on his way to the back room.

Chronic depression in shitty wellies.

I shadowed him to the garden pond. Spring air of early May. I was hoping it would revive him. And me.

Over the ramparts at number 5 Edenhurst, the white-haired neighbours were taking advantage of improved weather: Ted Barton mowing their lawn; Nelly, his wife, hanging out an extensive weekly wash before clouds drew in from the Lickey Hills. On noticing Mr O'Dowd and Enoch-the-Unmentionable-Absentee, they made a hasty move indoors.

'What's in the water?' said Mr O'Dowd, scribbling another price on his notepad.

'Fish.'

'Can't see a perishing thing.'

'Minnows and carp, I think. You'd have to use a net.'

'We'll dredge,' he said boldly. 'Don't you sweat.'

'You sell fish?'

'Someone'll eat 'em.'

The man's spirits had collapsed irrevocably. He sat for a moment on Vera's wooden bench. Laying aside the notes, he placed hands on knees and peered into blackwater. His gloomy expression moved me.

'Is everything okay, Mr O'Dowd?'

He gazed at the ripples as though deciphering messages. 'Fine, Mr Jones.'

'Only you look a bit peaky.'

'Do I?'

'We can take a break, you know. Would you like a drink of something?'

'Whisky?' he said, rather promptly.

'Yes, there *is* some.'

I brought him a glass and we stared at the pond. I glanced over at Ted Barton's ground zero mowing and at Nelly's skirts and blouses tripping about like a chorus line. Faces moved away from the Barton kitchen window.

'Maudlin, really,' he said after a few minutes.

He was coming out with it at last. I hoped it wasn't too bleak.

'Lost a Friesian,' he mumbled.

At first I didn't know what he was talking about.

'Started running backwards last afternoon. Squealing and snorting, she was. Then dropped down dead in the brook.'

Mr O'Dowd had lost a cow.

I had to keep calm. People lost dogs and hamsters all the time – and were accorded a most respectful understanding. Pets were family.

But a cow?

'I'm very sorry, Mr O'Dowd,' I said. This was my first experience of someone with a close personal relationship to a dairy animal. 'Had you known each other long?'

'Years. She wasn't like the others.'

What do you say next? She won't be a burger between someone's buns? Was that an unkind remark?

In some confusion, I looked up at the Barton house. Nelly and Ted had now shifted. From their back-bedroom window, two wintry heads showed above the netting. Like Friesians in a stall, really. How I wished *they* would start running backwards.

'I'll get over it, Mr Jones,' he said, slugging back the whisky. 'Just as you will your mother.'

'Enoch.'

'Enoch.'

'It's very painful to lose someone you love,' I suggested, getting into it. But sounding like Melissa Braithwaite.

He looked at me strangely. 'Not taking the piss are you?'

'Not at all, Mr O'Dowd. I know a great deal about loss, if you want the truth.'

'Sorry,' he said, standing up. 'The grief an' all.'

'I understand.'

Grief. Mr O'Dowd had helped me into darkness. Thank you, Mr O'Dowd. Memories – that gift as old as Methuselah – memories I'd rather have evaded, would have their fullest innings this time around.

O'Dowd held out his tumbler rather imploringly.

'Drop more?'

'Wouldn't hurt, would it?'

I waved hello to the Bartons upstairs as we strolled past the shed to the French door. I wouldn't want to be rude.

Ghost and shadow back inside; Mr O'Dowd following me to the whisky which, like much of the house, was inside a box in the hall.

Treasure Trove's thundercloud had lifted slightly by the time he'd quaffed a second Scotch and lit up yet another cigarette. I sensed he'd enjoy further drinks for the road, but truly this was enough. There was only so much road to prepare for. The listing of Vera's possessions – and the Friesian bereavement – had worn me down.

Mr O'Dowd stood by the front door – in light from a hall window – doing his final arithmetic with a stubby pencil, cigarette and smoke writhing between his dentures. 'Twenty-six, four hundred and ...'

Without a word and in great solemnity, at last he handed me a folded sheet of paper and turned away. Sums for the schoolmaster.

Cautiously – to accommodate his fragile state – I opened it as if handling one of those Shakespeare Folios – 'Seven hundred and seventy-five pounds, all found,' it read. 'Full house clearance for Mr Jones.'

Least it wasn't 666 in my face.

His calculations seemed fair enough. I was encouraged. This was the highest quote yet.

As I considered the offer, Mr O'Dowd grew impatient, as though he didn't know where to look, penned in between boxes.

All of a sudden – as I was about to accept the man's price – he inhaled a mammoth drag from his cigarette and ground it out in the urn: Vera's ashes innocently minding their own business on the window sill.

I gasped.

O'Dowd was startled – and fell back against the door, his stain of a nose ripening with alarm.

'I *know*,' he moaned, 'but what can I *do*?'

His forehead was shiny; he wrung his hands.

'No, no, Mr O'Dowd, it's okay,' I said, gazing from urn to the man's anguished face.

'Look,' he said, mustering his forces. 'Let's make it an *even eight hundred*. Eight hundred quid and the house cleared and scrubbed like a baby's bum?'

Clapping his hands, he made mincemeat of a deal.

'Fine, fine, Mr O'Dowd,' I said appeasingly, still mesmerized by the filter-tip poking out of my mother. 'Done.'

'Phew,' he said, mopping his brow with a handkerchief. 'I thought we'd lost you at the crucial moment!'

Mr O'Dowd grabbed my hand and shook it vigorously. There was a not ungritty dust on his fingertips – and now in my palm. He bounced down the slope towards his Land Rover.

'Saturday week do you?' he shouted, beaming. 'Nine?'

'Perfect!' I called back, brushing my fingers.

He must have been more accustomed to calling across acres of pasture than a Grove. Out in the road his personality was transformed. Had I been the one to make his mood darken?

'Cheerio then, Mr Jones!' he said, waving.

'What was her name, by the way?' I called out.

'Whose?'

'The dairy animal.'

'No name,' he replied.

'Just a pretty face, Mr O'Dowd?'

'Great flanks,' he roared back, winking.

Did I understand this man at all?

'Treasure Trove at your service, Mr Jones!' he bellowed, giving a forelock salute before leaping into the driver's seat. Buccaneer at his wheel.

I stared at the urn and closed the door.

'Don't say a dicky-bird,' I told Vera, reaching in and exhuming the cigarette nub. 'Be thankful it wasn't a cigar.'

I knew Vera would get a tickle out of Mr O'Dowd's using her as an ashtray. Just as she'd find her funeral a hoot – all those *Pinky and Perky* people scurrying to get her to the grill on time.

When she let herself enjoy it, Vera had the chirpiest sense of humour in all Longbridge. Wasn't this the best? For the first time since arriving in Birmingham, I missed the ancient baggage. A mountain-sized chuckle in that wronged life of hers.

I was hearing Vera at last. Wasn't I? Laughter? Giggling. The way she turned aside to bury it, clutching her skirt like a shy child.

Memories gained on me.

Before I could take a step further, tears stung my eyes.

For the rest of her days, Vera would have told neighbours up and down Edenhurst about Mr O'Dowd's cigarette. She'd have had them rolling in the aisles, I just know. Maybe there's love here somewhere, Ma. For that rare, perfect funny bone in you – another keepsake as old as Adam. Within the harshness and longing.

I stared at ash. Grizzled. Even a mad cow has its mourner, I thought. You mustn't fear the grief.

Along the skirting board lay more unopened letters, one from the Queen Elizabeth Hospital in Edgbaston. Couldn't be a bill, I thought. How curious. Vera was National Health to her pom-pom slippers.

Wiping my eyes, I tore it open and meandered to the back room. 'Dear Mrs Vera Jones,' it read. 'Following instructions from your consultant, it has become necessary to alter your appointment at Dr Piddick's Coronary Clinic. A new time has been arranged for Thursday September 22nd at 4:00 p.m. I hope that this does not cause you any inconvenience.'

Dr Piddick treated the living *and* the dead.

'Why not show up, Ma?' I said, tossing his letter into the empty fireplace and heading out through Vera's French door. 'Today, you were something else.'

PART TWO

THERE'S A COMMA AFTER 'LOVE'

Birmingham, England. 1966.

Ripped, cut off: all Dad's gear's like that. Yesterday night I'd been sitting in the back of our Austin Standard Eight, like I am this evening – three hours so far, outside the Saracen's Head – looking at his woollen mittens. He uses them for fishing. There's another two under the dash here. No fingers in *them*, either. When you stick your bare pinkies through, it's like upside-down underpants with leg-holes and one for the tiddler. So you tie hooks, floats and shot in them. It's easier to feel the bits that way. Dad rolls his Rizlas wearing a pair and picks bogeys like there's no tomorrow.

Everything.

Ties knots.

I watch his knuckles bob about.

I like watching him.

He should have worn them last night when Clara and Fanny, who are not my real aunts by the way, made him go berserk about his *signature*. Writing's difficult in these mitts, see. It's the wool. Much too thick for a pen. Mitts would have saved him, but he got caught out.

Gloves come off indoors.

It was the Peacocks car park yesterday evening. Foggy drizzle on the windows. Thursdays it's cod and chips and then the Pig and Whistle. Fridays: faggots and peas and the Jolly Fitter, Saturdays: bubble and squeak and the Peacocks. Sundays: bread and dripping and the Saracen's Head. Like clockwork.

So. Saturday night, and Ma and Dad were inside the...?

'Peacocks'! Right. I'd finished my Vimto and crisps hours

before, so I picked up the *Scout's Handbook*. Stupid really, because it was getting dark and Dad won't let me put the car light on.

Boy Scouts get up my nose, to tell you the truth. But I never say. Toy soldiers with nappies, aren't we, lighting fires and howling at each other? Sick. Tangled up in reef-knots and sheepshanks and simple whipping. Lashing poles together like Robinson Crusoe on a mission. Pukey, pukey.

I hate it all.

But Ma has ambitions for me. So I dug out a torch from under the old man's half-finger gloves and found a page called 'Scout Vocabulary: *Foreign Terms.*'

Great, I thought. Something that doesn't involve rope.

I tried it – writing with these underpant-mitts of Dad's – at Oddingley a fortnight ago, while he was weighing in along the Worcester canal. It was the huge annual Birmingham Anglers' Association contest, south-west of the city. Freezing cold, sunny Sunday morning. Oil patches on the water. Even on me the gloves were tight. Shows how shrunk the old man is.

Squirming about on his homemade creel I was, trying to keep warm while I practised joining a few letters together in an old Letts notebook.

What happened?

Well, my fingers cramped every time I tried to fiddle them into an adult – *longhand* – sentence. Kept sliding down the pen. I was doing a George-and-the-Dragon routine trying to write in longhand like a grown-up. Stabbing and stroking at the notepaper, twisting it and myself about.

Like Dad tying a hook.

What a mess. Zigzags all over the ruled lines like some heart attack, definitely a job for *Thunderbirds*, my favourite telly programme. I'm already eleven years old, I thought. How am I going to be ready for grammar school if I'm still printing letters one by one, like a junior?

I looked across the mucky water. Maybe it's like pubic hair, I thought. Really slow to turn up.

But I got visitors last night in the Austin Standard Eight. Parked outside the Peacocks for hours in that damp fog.

The first arrivals I pretty much asked for, I'd been staring at the pub's sign for too long. Drinking too much pop. I started imagining a quiz show with Dougal the dog and Mr Rusty from *Magic Roundabout* on the BBC. 'Ever had a *notfall*, Dougal?' I was yelling in our dithery scoutmaster Mr Wimbledon's voice, like we were in a parade ground or something. I don't know what was the matter with me, shouting.

'That's German,' I said. '*Notfall* means emergency.'

Dougal seemed unimpressed. I couldn't get him to notice me. I pictured him leaving his pal Mr Rusty, and taking Mr Wimbledon through Sainsbury's on a Saturday afternoon.

Our scoutmaster's a thirty-year-old schoolteacher who wears his beret and badges even in the supermarket. Dougal, with furry paws, was explaining to all the customers how Mr Wimbledon holds his neckerchief together with a phony, plastic toggle in the shape of a grizzly bear's head. You get a hell of a lot of grizzly bears in the city of Birmingham. *Forward* is the motto. Wildlife in a coat of arms.

All the shoppers applauded as Dougal pointed at Mr Wimbledon's toggle. Was the dog envious or what? In my mind I kept pulling at Dougal's collar, getting him to see *me*. 'I've passed the eleven-plus exam, Dougal,' I started yelling again, at the windscreen wipers now. 'I'm having a major *notfall*. If you're interested?' I wrenched the gear-stick from reverse to first, back and forth, sped the wipers up. 'Eleven-plus! What have I *done*?'

I imagined Mr Wimbledon shaking his head sternly. Dougal was standing at the checkout next to him like he was impatient, looking me dead-eye.

'Eleven-year-old boys face the cut-off, Enoch Jones,' he said doggedly. 'Grammar school one way. Secondary, the other. Leaping wolves have to leave Akela sometime.'

'Cubs join the Scouts,' said Mr Wimbledon, walking his shopping-cart out of the building as Dougal and I watched.

'We don't all end up like Mr Wimbledon, do we?' I asked, feeling concerned. Dougal wrinkled his nose. Headlights washed over me from the parking space opposite. A couple in their twenties climbed out and hurried inside the Peacocks.

Suddenly, 'Dyb, dyb, dyb,' sang Dougal, turning himself around and around. Bleating like a young Ringo Starr on helium. 'Dob, dob, dob,' he spluttered turning the other way, barely containing himself.

'Aw fuck off, Dougal,' I said, gazing into the rear-view mirror. 'Get on your riding-horse.'

When I turned around, there were two peculiar faces at the back window. Yes. There were more visitors. Strangers. But *not* in my head. Real visitors this time. In a panic, I dropped the torch.

The car door flung open. Light shone everywhere, blinding. Dougal's magic roundabout did a loop-the-loop in my head. I was stuck. Can't I touch the ground? Peacocks squawking, feathers in the air. Dougal tumbled onto Mr Rusty. Mr Wimbledon's toggle became a real bear. Chewing his own head. There *were* bears in Birmingham! I started to scream as two hands reached in to shut me down.

'*Notfall, notfall,*' I was shouting, kicking the fingers away.

'Enoch!' called Dad, jogging along the canal with his keepnet in the air. Wiry as he is, he's not a runner. 'Out o' mah way, lad!' His cheeks blotchy, breathing hiss-pop like a steam train. 'Out o' mah way, Enoch.'

The fish were wild, thrashing against the net, scales and water spraying across his jacket and on me.

My pen and pad fell into the reeds as he knelt beside me at the water's edge.

'Whoa, boys! Steady on!' Dad slithered in mud, shaking the last fish into the canal.

Their eyes were his eyes – and I stared.

'Oh Enoch. On your tod in the car again. My little dear.'

It was Fanny, one of my aunts-who-aren't-really. Her lip was trembling.

'What's wrong, Aunty Fanny?'

'We heard the news,' said Aunty Clara, behind. 'We're so happy! We've got a little surprise for you.' She was grinning, but it slipped away. 'Come out of that damn seat.'

'It's "last call" in there,' said Aunt Fanny, hugging me into her church-hall-smelly coat. She gestured at the Peacocks as though it were a curse on mankind. 'Your dad and mum'll be over to our caravan in a minute. We've invited them, too. Come along.'

Fanny's eyes looked sore.

Theirs is the last caravan in the row, down in a dell. Six down from ours. Every spring, bluebells and primroses shoot up all over their grass. That's how I see it *all* year, because they don't grow anything else.

Inside, heavy curtains and dark wood make their home seem like a real house. They practically frogmarched me in. I stopped, breathless, to pat their dog. He's a plaster of Paris cocker-spaniel: Sandsy. Life-size. Named after another lady officer like Aunty Clara, a famous one, called Flora Sandes. I always stroke her leg – the dog's – when I go in. Aunt Clara says that 'she' is a 'he'. And there he-she always sits upon a pedestal on the lemon-polished sideboard, smiling. Eyes following you everywhere, like in a famous painting.

'Isn't *Man from UNCLE* on television, Fanny? Maybe Enoch would like to watch it?' said Clara, trying to fit the poker back into its rack.

'No, dear,' Fanny replied, helping me out of my boots. 'He wants his surprise, don't you?'

'Well yes,' I said, looking all over the place. 'What is it?'

'Or *The Fugitive* or *The Saint*? *Thunderbirds*? Must be....'

'Clara, please. You get them so muddled.' She rolled her eyes and I sniggered. 'Enoch knows we have rules about TV, even if he's such a clever boy. Grammar school, my dear! Now tell me, which one will it be? Bluecoat School, King Edwards, or Solihull?'

Fanny staggered about on the rug, shaking my anorak dry. 'Oh heavens!' she cried as bundles of string – like intestines – tumbled out of the pockets. 'Look at this jumble!'

'Back into the drink!' Dad said, almost singing. He usually says that. 'Wee! There they go, son,' pointing into the darksome, still whiffing a trail the fish leave.

He loves the chucking-back, silver coins sinking away. He looks like a boy then – on his first day. The keepnet lies in the grass, tired out, all muscle gone.

You feel like you've done no harm.

'Silly me!' said Fanny stooping to gather the piles of string.

'Only my knots,' I said. 'For Scouts.'

'Let's see here,' said Clara, moving from the stove towards me. She usually knows what to do.

'It's okay. I can fix them, Aunty.'

But there's no stopping her. Clara was a soldier in the First World War – and an officer in the Second. 'I remember these bloody knots.'

Fanny pulls a face whenever Clara gets going on her army days. That makes me laugh, too.

She and Fanny seem quite elderly in their heavy skirts and stockings. But they might not be. It's hard to tell. They're both very plump, shuffling about and chattering, making the caravan creak like a boat.

Never in our trailer. Sometimes it's hard to believe anyone lives there. We don't seem to move much. Or speak.

Clara, by the way, does not sit down. Ever.

Suddenly there's a loud bang.

Clara at attention, glancing at Fanny.

Someone's hand sliding along the caravan.

Dad wiped his fingers on the grass and cleaned the rod-rest. 'Keep an eye on the maggots, did you, Enoch?'

'Here, Dad,' I said holding the container with its awl-pricked top.

'Good lad. Gotta watch those blighters. Get everywhere they will.'

From amongst the reeds I picked up the fallen pen and paper. As I bent down, I felt his fingers grip my neck.

'Not near the water, lad.'

He took the pad and pen from me, dabbed both with a rag and slipped them carefully – precious cargo – into his hand-carved box.

I gazed at him.

He'd never done anything like that. Handled my writing material so gently. Pen and paper in the creel on his back – a first – amongst quill floats with orange tips and Lincoln green tails. One of the lads. It was like Dad had invited me into the pub. I couldn't keep my eyes off him.

'Oh goodness,' said Fanny, waddling through the kitchen. 'Here are your parents.'

'Hello there, ladies!' My dad, bowing. He was drunk.

Showtime.

As I said, there's a lot about him that's way, way out. Mostly, he's a silent man, as if he's angry or scared. Never content. Then, like here in Clara and Fanny's caravan, he's all shakin'-a-baby-now, nattering ten to the dozen like he's the luckiest man on earth.

'Drinks for all,' announced Fanny opening a cupboard while Ma and Dad took off their coats. 'Then we'll give the boy his present.'

'You're a bother, our Enoch,' said my dad, wagging his finger once it was free of his raincoat, 'leaving the car unlocked like that. I dunno....'

'Sit yourselves down,' said Fanny as she set some bottles of beer on the table. 'Enoch was demonstrating some of his knots, weren't you dear?'

Dad took out his battered tin of AI. Started to roll. Clara, standing by the stove again, offered him a Park Drive.

'Don't mind if I do,' he said, snapping the tobacco tin shut.

She put one in her mouth and struck him an England's Glory.

'Well, that's a sheepshank,' said Clara, identifying one of the knots. 'Sheetbend, clove hitch, reef knot and ... what's this one?'

'Round turn and two half hitches,' I told her.

'Bingo!' she said, taking up a bottle of beer. 'You're the expert.'

'Don't we know it,' said Ma.

She doesn't smile often.

'I'm better at knots than lashing and simple whipping,' I said. 'I'm hopeless at tracking.'

Aunty Clara nodded.

'Next month I have to choose between axemanship or first aid.'

My dad belched and excused himself.

'First aid,' said Clara.

'*Then* axemanship,' said Fanny. 'It would be less of a worry for your parents, if you got hurt.'

Aunty Fanny always tries to make everything sound clear and sensible. Even if it's not.

'Scouts, new school,' said Clara. 'What a hair-raising time, Mr Jones.'

'Call me Frank, please.'

'Well,' Ma began.

'Expensive lark this grammar school,' he interrupted, looking at my aunts-who-aren't. 'Bit of a palaver.'

'One of the schools sent a list,' said Ma in her worried voice. 'Didn't they, love?'

'Don't ask me,' Dad replied.

'Rugby outfit, cricket, tennis,' she continued. 'Oxford dictionary, "macintosh for *inclement* weather", hymn-book. I tell you.'

Fanny glanced at Clara again.

'Got to get to the school every day too,' added my dad, 'from Bloxwich here. Not easy.' He took a long, fancy drag of his Park Drive.

'With you and Vera both working,' said Fanny, 'it won't be so bad, will it? Money-wise?'

'There's hire purchase at the department stores,' Clara said abruptly, as though it were shelter for her battalion. 'We'd love to buy the school tie, if you'll permit us.'

Ma looked embarrassed.

'We'll see, we'll see,' said Dad, turning to me. 'On the never-never ...' He took another gulp of beer. I wasn't used to his eyes on me. 'Now what's this little something you've got our Tommy Trouble?'

'We're all agog,' said Ma, hunching her shoulders like a Sunday-school girl.

'Is this homework in the creel, Enoch,' he said, lobbing some unused groundbait into the canal, 'what you've been writing?'

'I wrote down what Aunty Clara says every teatime, like "cheers" or "grub up". Look, Dad. Even when I'm not there, Clara says it. Fanny told me. Look.'

From my pocket I tried to show him the inky page I'd crumpled up. It read: 'To Our Three Selves.' I wished the O's were rounder.

'Longhand or printed?' he said quickly, tapping the breadcrumbs from his overalls. I looked at him. But he was concentrating on his hands. What was he saying? After last night at Clara and Fanny's caravan.

'Longhand *and* printing,' I said, trying to show him the mucked-up sheet.

Dad ignored the piece of paper as he secured the landing-net and rod in their canvas hold-all. 'Longhand's important now, Enoch.'

My stomach did a somersault.

'Yeah,' I said, trying to sound casual.

Aunty Fanny lumbered to the back of the caravan.

'One more?' said Clara.

'Don't mind if I do,' replied my dad.

Three of us sat quietly, like we were on the bus, while Clara dug about in a cupboard.

'Surprise!' cried Fanny, making her way from the bedroom. She handed me a small packet wrapped in red tissue.

'Another Corona pop, Enoch?' asked Clara.

33

It was so much more fun in *their* caravan.

'A Parker pen!' I said, opening the giftbox. 'Wow!'

Every day this month I'd seen the billboard on my way to school, and I'd told Fanny because I couldn't understand it. A boy in glasses is looking fed up. 'I hate my best friend,' it says. 'He may have a Parker 61, but he can't talk proper!'

Now I did have a Parker. I jumped up and hugged Fanny and Clara.

'You shouldn't have,' said Ma. Her face looked serious. 'It's a beauty.'

'That it is,' agreed my old man.

Fanny laid out a card with 'Thank Your Lucky Stars' on the front. I was hoping Ma and Dad weren't going to shout when we got home. They didn't think it a good idea for children to receive gifts over the eleven-plus exam. 'It's bribery,' Dad had explained, when my schoolmate Gary got a bike.

'That's it, Enoch,' said Fanny. 'You write your name and we'll all do the same. As a memento.'

'Write a wish, too,' Clara added. 'So we all can see.'

I'd been practising signatures for weeks. This was *the* moment.

Dad was smirking. I couldn't work out why. He led off along the canal towpath with his creel and tackle, cinders crunching beneath his waders. I followed with empty keepnet. We passed a decrepit-looking bridge – number 26. Red brick.

Then it dawned on me.

'Have you won anything in the fishing contest, dad?'

He turned slightly.

'Have you, dad?'

'Look, Ma. I can sign my name.'

'Very good, Enoch,' she said, impatiently. 'Now write your wish like Aunty Clara says.'

Carefully I joined the letters, curve by curve, into a flow that more or less made it. Finishing, I looked up at everyone, then back at the handwriting: 'Enoch Jones. The Scout smiles and whistles under all difficulties.' From printing letters to *this*. With a Parker 61. I was full of it. Didn't really think about what I was writing.

'Elegant hand, my boy.' Fanny held up the card and showed it to Clara and my parents. 'What a standard you've set us Black Country spinsters.'

'That's not a wish,' said Ma. 'A Scout smiles and whistles ...'

'It's a watchword, perhaps?' interrupted Clara. 'More than enough for the eleven-plus.'

'You sign now, Aunty Fanny.'

So she did. Then Ma, then Clara. Each signature followed by a message I couldn't see upside down.

'We should be off,' said Ma, laying down the pen in its velvet box. 'Get your anorak, Enoch.'

'Let's not forget *Dad's* John-Henry,' responded Clara, pushing the card his way.

'Wife's taken care of it, haven't you love?'

'Yes, I have.'

'Fetch your coat then,' Dad told me.

I headed for the cupboard to find it.

'No, no, Frank,' I heard Fanny say as she retrieved the pen. 'You *must.*'

'We can do it later Fanny,' said Ma, standing. 'It's well past Enoch's bedtime.'

'We *insist.*' Clara touching the 'Lucky Stars'.

Dad sighed.

As I turned with my coat, he snatched up the card.

Under the canal bridge, Dad tapped his nose and indicated a path we should follow along the embankment.

'Dad? Tell me.'

'Eight pounds, nine ounces, four drams, Enoch,' he said, as I hurried to keep up.

'That's lots of fish!'

'One hundred and twenty-five pounds, seventeen shillings and threepence.'

He patted his back pocket.

I returned to the table wearing my anorak. Dad was sweating. His hand moved slowly, like he was tracing something important.

Clara stoked the fire.

Fanny watched him and then looked at me very sternly. Ma pushed past. She didn't look very pleased, either.

'Son, your mother's coat's on the seat down there. And your father's. Will you pick them up, please?'

'Here, Ma,' I said, holding out their macs.

'Very thoughtful of you both to buy him a present,' she repeated. It sounded so unlike my mum, all this thanking. 'Enoch, you take care of the pen, now. He's always losing things.'

'A small ceremony,' said Fanny, 'for such an important exam.'

I held out Dad's coat for him. We all stood waiting for the old man to complete his own name. Fanny looked at me and pulled a daft face. Just like she does with Clara's World Wars.

I laughed.

'Come on, slowpoke,' I said. '*I'm* quicker than you, Dad. Aren't I, Ma?'

'*Love Dad*' he had written. Carefully twisting a full stop – like a skewer – into the page.

'That's first prize, Dad! You've won first prize!'

I caught hold of his sleeve and he shook me off.

'You wait till we tell Ma!' I shouted, doing a hop, skip and a jump. 'Thunderbirds are GO!'

'Bit of cash, ain't it?' he said, struggling over the stile with all his tackle, 'for that mother of yours.'

We were the last to leave, and with a coach to find.

Oddingley's canal undisturbed once more.

'Congratulations, Dad,' I sang out, looking back at the water.
'Put a stopple in her, eh Enoch?'

'What about the wish then?' I asked my dad. 'I want a wish.'
'You'll get one later,' said Ma. 'Plus a fat ear. Let's be going.'
'A long wish, Dad,' I went on. 'And there's a comma after
"*Love*".'

'You keep it down, Enoch Jones,' said Ma, shaking me. 'You're
tired and it's late. Aunty Fanny and Aunty Clara want to go to bed.'

'Not me, Vera,' said Clara. 'You write on, Frank Jones.'

Dad looked up at Ma. Then again, like a child, he bent over the
card. She glanced at the two-aunts-who-aren't and sighed just as
Dad had done. So I did the same.

'Full sentence,' I added.

He didn't reply. I went over to stroke Sandsy, killing time.

Suddenly there was an ear-splitting yell. Like someone hurt
badly.

My dad.

Then a clattering sound against the caravan wall. Sandsy almost
came to life beneath my hand.

My dad. He was on his feet. 'Bastards!' he was screaming. 'Bastards, bastards!' There was a line of ink all down the curtain. 'Let
me outa here!' He knocked past a table.

Fanny was holding out the ink spots staining her blouse, touching them with her finger. Dad rushed out the door. There was ink on
Clara's face too.

'Quick march, young man,' said Ma, yanking me outside.

'I'm sorry,' I replied, noticing my sploshed card still open on the
table. 'What did I do?'

'So you should be. He's your *father*, you ungrateful ...' Ma
began.

'What about the pen?' I said. 'Dad threw my pen!'

But Ma had grabbed my ear.

'He doesn't know how to *write*, you silly swine.'

Suddenly I hated her and him. Everyone. Why hadn't anyone

told me? Even these fatties provoking something in me I didn't fully understand. This was another *notfall* wasn't it? Real one. We were in the middle of a living *notfall*. Fuck, I thought. *Notfall! Notfall!*

'Frank, you rattlehead,' said Ma as we headed up the field behind Natsfield Farm.

'They're like that murderer, Myra Hindley. The two o' them,' he said.

'Don't be a clod, man. They mean well.'

'You keep the lad away,' he ordered. 'You hear? Lezzies, those women.'

'What?' said Ma.

'You heard,' he snapped. 'Lesbians, funny peculiar.'

'They love our Enoch. What the hell's wrong with that?'

'Need all the help they can get,' he went on, opening our gate. 'Women like them.'

'Oh Christ, Frank.'

'They're not picking on our nipper, love.'

'You're the real donkey's arse. Know that?'

Once inside our plot, he started kissing Ma like he wanted to eat her face. It didn't sound right. Ma kept trying to speak.

So I ran back. We hadn't even said good night to Clara and Fanny.

But it was too late. Only the bedroom light was on.

I stood on my tiptoes. Fanny was in her bra holding the stained blouse. She was shaking her head. Clara came into the room and slipped her arms around Fanny's fleshy waist. Now they were finding something amusing.

Fanny took out a handkerchief.

I didn't really understand why everyone got so annoyed.

As I walked back up the field, I became nervous. Even thought about taking a stroll along the Wyrely-Essington canal near our site. I started whistling the *Avengers* theme tune. Was the problem Dad's writing so slowly? He didn't finish his sentence. Or was it the gift of a fancy pen? You never knew with grown-ups; they were always so on edge.

The lights weren't lit in our caravan, but the door was open. I could hear Ma laughing, just like Fanny and Clara. Maybe it wasn't that important after all. So when I stepped into the darkness, I smiled too – just like they tell you to do in that silly handbook – even though my insides felt like the tightest reef-knot Baden-Powell ever knew.

I kept on whistling.

They'd know I was back.

'Here.'

I handed Dad the fishy mitts he'd dropped on the towpath, and gate-vaulted the stile to follow him over Oddingley's railway tracks.

'Thanks, love,' he said as though speaking to Ma, hurrying across the main Birmingham-Bristol line. Forget the level crossing. In his thoughts he was already home in Bloxwich – other side of town – flush with the day's winnings. I looked right, left and right again for him and for me.

'Wait, Dad!' I yelled.

But he was through a hawthorn hedge on the other side, before I'd even started, like a finger through that mitt.

LESSONS IN SPACE

At Christmas I stole a blue diary from Woolworth's in Bloxwich.

I wanted to pin down a few things in my seventeenth year. Exams in the summer, there'd be exams – O levels – and from then? *A Test for Life* they called it on the box. But today, according to this diary, it's Ascension Day. I forget what that means – religiously speaking – but, boy, have I had a *rise*. Written, 'Had my first shag ever. Must do it again!' At the top of the page, in addition to some vertical dashes (to indicate wanks), I've drawn two horizontal lines, like an equals sign, that meet the vertical ones. Contact, you see? Secret code in case Ma goes snooping.

With a black felt tip, I've also put 'Ear infection – and Uncle Graham – worse. But if Commander Shepard can get over a ten-year earache, and fly to the moon in Apollo XIV, then so can I. Am ignoring the ringing in my head – and Uncle Graham. The old lady's very upset, miscounts the new decimal currency all over again, and wears peach a lot with those tinny-looking earrings that whirl like radar. Dreading Sunday.' There's not much room on the page for anything else, except Word for the Week. I try to use posh ones from a mildewed dictionary I found at Natsfield Farm auction.

'Tumescence,' I've scribbled. 'Beats "a boner" by miles.' I'm not sure what I meant by that last bit, now I look at it. Anyway. Tumescent. I wonder how people use the word? I am tumescent, you are tumescent. *She* is tumescent? Can you have that? Well, if Ma does read all this, she won't know what tumescent means, so who's worrying.

That's my diary for Ascension Day – Enoch Jones's seventeenth year.

To tell you the truth, the past few months have been pretty ampullaceous, too. Get that? It's my Word for Easter week. It's like tumescent but it's got something to do with bottles – and there are plenty of those where I come from. Ampullaceous. It's like being uncorked. That's how I feel here, sometimes – at this Black Country caravan site on the Wyrley-Essington canal. A genie trying to burst out, or like Apollo xiv. The trouble comes when you try to get back inside, though. Into the bottle again. Because you've seen what's *outside*.

Back in February, a few weeks before my sixteenth birthday, I was watching a tv program on space missions. What else do you do on a windy Sunday morning? Apollo xiv was on its flight to the moon. Normally I wouldn't give a toss. But the commentator was interviewing some scientist who was saying they should call it Dionysus xiv because there'd been so many problems. I didn't follow everything he said, but I liked the shots of pipeclay men floating away from a spaceship, silver cords hanging from their bodies. Earth below.

All the time, I was figuring how to get out of the driving lesson with Uncle Graham who – like our neighbours Aunty Clara and Fanny – is no *real* relative. For some reason, we don't have any. He and my ma had become pals at New Year and I don't think Dad really appreciated that. I'd heard our Bealeys Lane milkman tell Aunty Fanny that Graham, the new arrival at Natsfield, was a jailbird. I don't know if that's true. People make up all kinds of stories. I think it's *Dad's* job to give me driving lessons, though. But obviously he can't, seeing as we don't have a car. So Uncle Graham it is.

'Can you help?' said Ma, as astronauts wafted about in the corner of our caravan. 'Buggers've got me.' She was awash in coloured sheets. Graph paper with football teams on one side and on the other a picture of two men tackling each other during a match. At the bottom, betting prices.

'You should get a calculator,' I told her, 'like this one.' I showed her the plastic wheel I'd lifted – also from Woolworth's – at Christmas. It looked like a space station but without the arms and legs. 'Tells you everything in the new currency,' I said. 'Works like a slide rule, except it's round.'

'Explain that again, Enoch,' she replied, shooing it away and pulling a face. She can look like a golliwog sometimes, the one on the jam jars. Except that Ma's hair is piled higher, and dyed. Her face shiny like a scrubbed hand. 'You have to keep telling me, that's all. It'll sink in eventually.'

As I went over the technique of converting two shillings into ten new pence, Ma painted her nails amber.

She doesn't like big changes. This month the country goes decimal. To Vera Jones, replacing pounds, shillings, and pence with 'one-hundred-pennies-in-a-pound' is like being told to drive on the other side of the road. Not that we have a car, like I said. But the *chaos*. Ma's reaction to this, as in all things, is to hang on tight – dress up a lot – hoping the threat will pass. But it's like putting on a spacesuit to fetch the groceries. It's overload. In the end, she gets everything so topsy-turvy that she's paralyzed, but great to look at.

'See,' I said, pointing to one of her customers' forms. 'Four pounds, three shillings and sixpence becomes' – I twisted the satellite – 'four pounds, seventeen and a half pence.'

'Give me the smokes, Enoch,' she replied, shaking her fingers to dry the lacquer.

Ma flicked a cigarette lighter and glanced at the evil wheel. I hoped her fingernails wouldn't go up in flames.

'Look.'

'Seventeen and a half pence,' said she, putting on a BBC accent. 'They're doing me everywhere I go, Enoch. Do you know that?'

Their decimals, *their* world, *their* money.

She studied the calculator a while longer. Frowned her taut, gloomy frown. But Vera Jones was enjoying these troubles. They were no match for the worry that usually beset her: my dad, Frank.

Since Ma had landed a part-time job delivering football pools door-to-door, she'd been pretty steady, enjoying the rituals. It got her away from tabloids and TV and helped her forget who she was married to. On Wednesdays, while Dad was welding one frame after another at the bicycle factory – night shift – she'd follow her usual route, to the caravans on our site behind Natsfield Farm, then to the proper homes on Bealeys Lane.

On Thursdays and Fridays she'd visit the ones she'd missed. Back home by ten or eleven, she'd be chatting about neighbours, her pockets stuffed with pound notes, pools sheets, and loose change. That's how she met Uncle Graham. He was a postman – on strike at present. Moved here the same day we did. They must have got talking. Ma's never very organized, and he probably helped her out.

Vera Jones is quite a looker – pulchritudinous is the way the library's jumbo dictionary puts it. Men usually take advantage of her ... pulchritude, I suppose. Sounds odd, doesn't it? So do her employers. She's no sense of using looks to *her* advantage. Ma's slow to catch on ... to anything. When the football pools company changed its rules slightly, for example, she was stunned.

It meant learning something new.

Pools are simple enough. You have to bet on which soccer teams will *draw* in their Saturday games, and you put an X by the team name. It took her weeks to understand the difference between 'score draws', 'goalless draws', and 'home and away wins' and the points that went with them. But she cottoned on eventually. The prizes were hundreds of thousands of pounds. Ma liked that. Even though no one she knew had ever won a farthing.

Real trouble started when the company introduced 'Spot the Ball' on the reverse side of the pools' sheets. It was a photograph of a moment in one of the previous week's football matches. The ball had been air-brushed out. For what used to be sixpence a go – 'a tanner on the ball wins you a fall' – you put an X where you thought the ball really was. Some jokers used to put two X's on a player's shorts. But that wasn't the right answer.

For Ma, with no head for numbers or much else, the problem was not only adding up the totals of crosses for the teams that might draw. She also had to count the number of 'Spot the Ball' crosses; then convert everything into decimal currency. Sixpence a go, for instance, became two and a half pence. What kind of slogan could you find for *that*? Besides, fractions to my ma were like something Americans call petty crime. Not worth the bother.

Most people, husbands mainly, helped her out, so she said. Wives were less tolerant. 'Oh these changing times,' I imagined her saying. 'So difficult keeping track these days' – all in her affected county lady's accent, the waxy grin, especially for Bealeys Lane. Ma thought customers would cancel if they found out she lived in one of the Natsfield caravans. So she spoke 'houseowner', as she put it, 'educated with time on my hands'. Sociably toothy. But her wedding-cake hair-do didn't help. Or the overdressing. It was too wilful. I'm sure people sussed her out.

Ma got home later and later. Worried someone would complain. Someone did.

My dad. He beat her up one teatime, and she got cabbage and Flora margarine all round her cheek. Then he went and smashed Uncle Graham outside the Man in the Moon at Bloxwich precinct. In the pub there'd been talk about Ma and Uncle Graham, he told me half apologetically.

But she still collected the pools each week. Uncle Graham gave me driving lessons. Dad never says much, but after that particular fight he signed off completely. Not a peep from the bloke. Something final had been decided. There was no going back.

Just beforehand, I met Stella at the Birmingham Hippodrome. She's my girlfriend of four months and she gives me tips on how to cope with Uncle Graham and my dad. I crashed into her on the stage of a rock musical, *Hair*.

I'd heard about the show because of Mrs Hikarius, our general studies teacher at Bournbrook Grammar School. She was getting us to read what she called the quality newspapers – *Daily Telegraph*, *Times*, *Guardian* (all the fancy ones with bear-hug sized pages) – instead of the *Sun*, *Mirror* and on Sundays the scandal-porn *News of the World* or the *People*.

What an eye-opener.

This *quality* world was a whole new one to me, not to mention all the nudie shows I was missing down in London: *Oh! Calcutta*, *Pyjama Tops*, *Abelard and Heloise*. Thank God for general studies

45

teachers like Mrs Hikarius. These newspapers reviewed everything – in long, wide paragraphs, with pictures. That's how I knew what *Hair* was about and that it was coming north. Like oxygen.

In its finale, the *Hair* cast invited us all on stage. Stella was dancing in the wings. I felt a right noddy letting the sunshine in, as the song says, with those tie-dyed people. Tripping about in bare feet, with plastic flowers around my neck. I didn't really know anything about the Age of Aquarius, nor about astrology, the Seventh House, or what happened when Jupiter aligned with Mars. But I soon got fired up and twirled about like a charlie, along with everyone. Then I collided with Stella.

'That's a weird dance!' she shouted.

In an hormonally charged, onstage frenzy, I'd been trying to imitate the opening petals of a sunflower at dawn. You can appreciate the difficulty.

'I'm flabellating,' I replied, petal left, petal right.

'What?'

'Flabellating,' I said. 'Fanning.'

I stretched my arms and fingers into an arc. I must have looked ridiculous because she started giggling. This was my latest Word of the Week; and here I was trying to dance it. What a freak.

Flabellating.

I liked Stella, her long black skirt with a fringe and the rainbow beads that bobbed over her nipples. She had a full face, pale in spite of all the jiving. She smelled of lavender and Pond's cream.

Outside the Hilton Grill, Stella began praising the tune 'Walking in Space' because it made her spine tingle. 'So much hope in that song, Enoch.' I told her I preferred 'What a Piece of Work Is Man' – I knew it came from Shakespeare somewhere, because it said so in the programme. To be honest, I liked the nude scene best, before the interval. But you try to impress a girl.

With eye-pencil, she wrote her number on my thumb and I gave her the Natsfield address. We don't have a phone. By the time we finished all that, and I'd kissed her, she took the last bus home to Edgbaston. I'd missed mine, of course. Walking in space back to

Bloxwich, hopping about those white lines in the middle of the road, I felt the *quality* Mrs Hikarius wished for us. Verses spilling from my mouth like someone cut adrift.

Five o'clock, back at our caravan, I wrote in the blue diary, 'Have flabellated myself into love. Stella is my girlfriend and we'll probably go to bed. Where do I get the johnnies? "Luminary" is the Word for Tonight. It's all yours, Stella. My ear infection is ringing off the hook with spaced-out songs from *Hair* at the Hippodrome. |||

'My ma's having it off with Lord Fiske,' I told Stella when we next met, on a Saturday night. We were on her parents' living-room floor.

'What do you mean, Enoch?'

She was wearing a see-through blouse. It reminded me of one of Ma's net curtains, but air-force blue and a hell of a lot more interesting to look through.

'Haven't you heard of him?'

'The decimal man?'

'Yeah.'

'Your old woman and Lord Fiske, Enoch. Come off it.'

'I've seen her.'

'Bollocks.'

'True, Stella. Ma goes out to the phone booth nearly every night.'

'So?'

'She keeps calling him.'

'What for?'

'Guy's a real slag, Stella. Gets calls day or night. Women and men.'

She shook her head.

'Look, Stella,' I said. 'Do you have a quality newspaper?'

'A what?'

'*Times*, Stella,' I replied. '*Telegraph*. Something like that.'

'Dad gets the *Daily Express*.'

She handed over a copy from beneath a cushion. I wasn't sure whether the *Express* was a rag or a posh one, but never mind. I found the full page advertisement and held it up. It was a picture of Lord

Fiske, chairman of the Decimal Currency Board, giving advice about Decimal Day. D-Day he called it, with telephone numbers for a free message from the peer himself.

'Gobshite,' she said.

But to me the Lord Fiske announcement was like a Wanted – Dead or Alive poster for Uncle Graham who was screwing my mum in his caravan. I didn't have the guts to tell Stella. That he was tearing my mum away from Dad, boring bugger that he is. It's funny how a harmless joke lets out pieces of the truth. Like some kind of one-armed bandit. Stella must have thought I was round the bend. It didn't stop her from jumping my bones, though.

Next Saturday too. Humpity hump. Stella's folks were out ballroom dancing, so we made out on the carpet during *Dixon of Dock Green* which came before the *Cilla Black Show*. BBC was the channel to watch, according to Mrs Hikarius. Stella and I never really did it. We got very close – worth a vertical line in the blue diary, but not a definitive 'equals' sign. Not yet. Besides, we stopped snogging when Cilla came on. It didn't seem right to be petting when she sang things like 'You're My World'.

One of these Saturdays was full of interruptions on BBC because Apollo XIV was on its way to that moon. The commentator getting agitated with technicalities. There had been more and more problems: Kitty Hawk, the command module, had made six attempts at docking with Antares, the lunar module. Some scientist was saying, 'The lunar probe hit the drogue' – Drogue! I grabbed that for a Word – 'at the dead centre every time we tried to make contact. It just rebounded off it.' He sounded very ernest trying to explain 'harddocking'. Stella and I couldn't keep our faces straight.

So while Kitty was failing to get it into Antares, some celebrity author was saying that 'the average American man, woman, and child paid $20 a year to finance Apollo, compared to an average of $180 per year on cigarettes, beer and liquor.' Stella and I couldn't get his point. What if Antares didn't like Kitty poking at it, she said? Did the expense justify a rape? Nothing's wrong with smoking and drinking instead. Mr Author sounded more and more like a cheerleader for something going very wrong.

All this space talk lost me my boner. So we got dressed and sat up for *Match of the Day*, wondering whether next week we should play 'Spot the Ball' on one of Ma's pools sheets. Somehow, during the game, we got onto Uncle Graham and the driving lessons.

'I let the clutch out too fast,' I told Stella.

'Bad,' she replied.

'That's when he grips my leg.'

'Oh.'

'He holds on, Stella.'

'So?'

'I shake him away. But he never goes.'

Stella was watching. I felt embarrassed saying.

'Did you tell your parents?'

'Ma.'

'Punch him in the gonads, Enoch.'

Why didn't I? 'I guess I'm scared of him.'

'What did your mum say?'

'I'm exaggerating. That I should let the clutch out more slowly.'

'Blimey.'

'Graham would never do anything like that, she says. Besides, I'm old enough to look after myself.'

The soccer crowd was chanting.

'Do you like what he does, Enoch?'

Why would she ask that?

'Don't be stupid.'

But Word of Last Week was in the air – 'equivocation', Uncle Graham's and my own. Uncertainty, butterflies and double meanings.

Someone scored a goal on *Match of the Day*.

'Do what they do in *Hair*, Enoch,' she said.

'Drug him, Stella?'

'Strip off. Stop the car in a busy place. Take off all your clothes. He won't touch you again. People like Graham get spooked when you show them more of what they want. In public.'

'Are you serious?'

'Deadly, Enoch.'

We were back to Apollo XIV all of a sudden. I imagined my striptease in town. New Street Station? Corporation Street? Bull Ring Centre? Could be a knockout. Meanwhile, the bloke on TV was pointing to a moon map and describing the Ocean of Storms. Behind him was a replica of 'MET – a modularized equipment transporter. That's a mouthful, eh?' said the man with perfect teeth. 'But to you and me it's a wheelbarrow. This is what Shepard will use during his moonwalk. Something we all employ in our backyards.'

'Man,' said Stella. 'We get to the moon and pull out a wheelbarrow. Sometimes we don't get very far, even if we do call it a modularized whatnot, do we, Enoch?'

Words of the Week were collapsing.

Seeing as it's Thursday evening, as well as Ascension Day, Ma is getting ready to collect pools money. She's going to wear a mauve anorak over all the white, plus red running shoes to look more sporty. It's hardly Aston Villa's colours, but it's closer than usual. She's been following all kinds of games, recently. It started with cricket when a seagull got hit by an Australian batsman's ball during the Sixth Test Match in Adelaide. She was on alert for further casualties. Then when Geoffrey Boycott threw his bat in the air and caused an international incident, you couldn't drag her away from the screen. Vera gets excited when order breaks down – that's why she loves weather reports in winter – it's as though she's drawn to disaster, but finds it frightening at the same time. Like living with my dad Frank.

Ma's right into soccer now: Aston Villa, of course. She knows all the names and thinks the team'll make the League Cup Final. She doesn't like the Blues because their colours put her off. Too bland. But Dad did get a shock when she started talking football. Pity he left her for good, next morning. They'd almost had a conversation. Dad said more that day than when they changed his pub from Man in the Moon to Man *on* the Moon – and he was beside himself then.

It's great for Ma's pools too – all this know-how. Even though she still can't count properly, she's got the lingo finally. Wives must dread her visits.

While I'm waiting for my beans on toast, I've drawn lots of vertical lines joined to equals signs all around today's page in the blue diary. They look like those space modules – or stars – but we really only did it once, Stella and I. Side of the Bloxwich gasworks there's a kind of shed. With the windows broken, it seemed a bit outdoors. Fantastic. I'm still looking for a Word to describe it. But I'll have to go to the Central Lending Library to get a truly mega-monolithic one that even Mrs Hikarius wouldn't recognize.

Two weeks ago, Uncle Graham paid a visit. No *Hair* stripdown up-yours thing, but I got a message across. As usual he was late, and my dad was sleeping off a night at the Moon. Uncle Graham never knocks. His face was at the caravan window – peering through the glass. Another man in the moon! Ma at the launderette.

I walked up to the door. Looked at his eyes like I did in the car, once he'd got us to park for a quiz on the Highway Code. I always wanted him to stop what he was doing. He never looked at me directly in that driver's seat, just down at his hand in my fly. I even felt sorry for him sometimes. But today I *had* him. I knocked on the glass and crossed one wrist over the other, hexing him like some demon or a witch. He scoffed at it, but moved back, gesturing me outside. I shook my head. He left. Bye-bye, Uncle Graham, the ten bob hushmoney along with him.

Not that brave, was it? But it worked. I learned the technique from my folks. We never really talk about anything until someone hits a bird on the TV or drops a bat. We kind of gaze, dumbly one day, threateningly the next. Normally, I would have preferred to use words, but with Uncle Graham my eyes were voice enough.

I'd like to write in the blue diary – for Ascension Day – that we never saw Uncle Graham again and that I get lessons from my dad. But there's no room on the page for anything else. Besides, it wouldn't be true. Off the page, it'd be great to say, like Commander Shepard when he stepped on the moon, 'It's been a long way, but we're here.' I'd love to say that – something ... tumescent. But it wouldn't be accurate.

Then there's Dad's postcard from Dagenham, where he's living now. A picture of the Wright brothers – Orville and Wilbur – and their flying machine back in 1903 as it's taking off from Kill Devil Hills. Dad must have looked for it specially. Under the brown and white image, it says, 'Flyer I, popularly known as Kitty Hawk, stayed in the air for twelve seconds on its first flight, fifty-nine seconds on its fourth and last.' Kitty must have been drinking its milk. I read this postcard a lot and keep it in the diary. Dad's even signed it and tells me – in longhand – that he's made new friends at the works. Sentence and a signature. Progress in the Frank department.

To be honest, it's been Lord Fiske from the Decimal Currency Board who's come through for me. On D-Day, when people like my ma had to get it right – or else – he said on his recorded message that Decimal Day was the non-event of the year. But what stays with me is his advice one night in the phone box, 'If in doubt, give more and get change.' That's how I feel about a lot of things now.

Like I said with 'ampullaceous', it's like I've burst out of a bottle and there really is no way back. So you shoot, shoot, shoot. Spot the Enoch! Moon-traveller. Letting the clutch out too fast in my seventeenth year. Space on a page full of crosses, where everyone's laid a bet.

HEAVEN

A few months before I was due to leave for Blanchland House, I started to play around again. Nicking stuff. Don't ask why.

It kept me going while I waited for the court-imposed sentence to begin.

Worked like a coke rush. Easy pickings all round. On Sunday nights.

My stepfather, Graham, was in the pub – the Jolly Fitter across from St. John the Baptist. Ma – Vera – was at home wailing along to 'Songs of Praise'. Once her piety was over for the Day of Rest – holy communion at eight-thirty of a Sunday morning, family service at eleven – she could resume what she'd been doing with Graham every Friday and Saturday night since we arrived in Longbridge from Bloxwich, a stone's throw from Birmingham's sprawling Austin Motor Company: at the bar until closing, 'never more than a rum and orange'.

To make herself feel holier, she'd enrolled me in the church choir.

St. John the Baptist was a naked place – heavily polished lily-white pine work and bleached walls. The building smelled of honey not to mention elbow grease Mrs Fidgeon worked off on its maintenance and 'floral improvements'. To my nose it was tutti-frutti.

Every Sunday morning, I churned out hymns, and Ma would appraise the congregation. She never missed a trick: attended coffee mornings, socials, jumble sales, Scout and Cub bazaars. Girl Guide and Brownie bingo nights. Christian Fellowship of England Club. You couldn't fault her for trying to blend in. But Ma had all the regulars down pat. According to her, no one passed the rinse cycle.

With their dowdy coats and cheap velvet hats, the women of St. John's were, according to Vera, 'gormless to a bunion – sooner they climb into their litter boxes the better.' Men didn't count – 'Most of 'em are women, anyway,' she'd say.

Yet Ma spent more time with the *harridans* – those dour God-fearing ladies – than with anyone in her life, even Graham. She detested the parishioners – men and women alike – no matter how kindly they behaved.

But I don't believe she ever troubled herself to ask why. What was wrong? Did we look different? Was it our accents, from a canal-side rural area only thirty miles away near Bloxwich? Were we gypsies selling clothespegs? Or had someone, once too often, put Vera down? Found those girlish, social ways too stagy? Who knows why newcomers didn't fit in. Ma sold football pools for *our* living. Graham was on the dole. *They* were all bricklayers', plumbers' and carpenters' wives. Austin car people. *Skilled*.

Ma wanted out, that's my guess, but didn't know where else was better. So Vera and Graham went on being the cheeriest outcasts in all Longbridge, doors closed all around. She ingratiated herself, never inviting a parish soul into our home. Nor they us into one of theirs. Except Nelly Barton next door – and she was heathen.

Church was like living at our council house in Edenhurst Grove. Infiltrators, we were. Fear hovering beneath every confident gesture. Upbeat pass-bys on the stairs and in the cramped hallway. Masks. None of us daring to speak honestly about our lives, what we really felt. Questions we yearned to ask. No wonder my philosophy blossomed at wanking and levelling war veterans for the life savings hidden in their squirrel teapots (hence the magistrate's sentence). What the hell did it take to turn my family circus off? Find some tenderness in our eyes? An honest word?

Wrongness loomed large over Edenhurst Grove, like David and Goliath entwined. One face ignoring the other. Not surprisingly, I was ready to explode.

I'd been at St. John's forever. Three months chanting and prattling my adolescence away. But after the business with the magistrate, Ma discreetly asked the vicar if I could join the senior choristers for weddings and funerals, held on Saturdays, as well as the two

Sunday services and evensong at six-thirty. A weekend of knee-blistering Protestant devotion, not to mention the choir practices of a Monday and Wednesday night. Shrouded in her guilt over my criminal lapse, I was heading for a bishopric. Some spiritual high for the damnation surely to follow at Blanchland House.

Reverend Langston Garnett from Bradford via Bloxwich – 'a meddling wog and the oddest you'll ever meet', as Ma liked to put it behind his back – had not hesitated. Or so she said. They always needed a good alto. Moreover, he'd offered to counsel her 'delinquent Enoch' if I had *need*. Reverend Garnett would pray for me. Of course, the circumstances would be safe with him. Not a word to anyone about reform school or Borstal. 'This is Longbridge, Mrs Jones,' he had said – meaning 'a cut above any place you've known to date and compassionate about its downtrodden' (although he didn't say that part). He would expect me for three Sunday services – no monies paid – and would enrol me in the Catechism Group for Young Britons. Help on that yellow brick road to enlightenment.

There went Tuesday and Thursday nights! Up in more chants and responses. Nothing like routine – with a chorus – to purify the damned, I thought. The whole thing stank of abuse. You should have seen the other devotees around the table. Vera would have cracked up: blubberbods, spinsters, a 'born again' Cub mistress and an alcoholic factory worker who saw existence in terms of assembly lines. Some hippy drug-bust from Northfield Lending Library. I was immersed in the holy.

Knives were drawn over the matter of Sunday at six-thirty, however: evensong at St. John's.

Nobody in the choir – except old-timers – enjoyed this hour-long excruciation of canticles and psalms. With a congregation of five or six widowed pensioners and an occasional refugee from the Jolly Fitter, this was the low point of St. John's week, illuminated solely by candles that trembled from many a draught in the hold – and from the merciless gaze of a certain Mr Ketland, the new and exemplary church warden who seemed especially devoted to pearl-faced boy choristers.

Even Reverend Garnett seemed deflated by it all – or was this *faith?* – particularly as he refused to allow heating until December ('the numbers don't warrant'). Then Mr Swithin, organist and choirmaster, who simply used the nocturnal occasion to rehearse his frenzied Bach, scratching his buttock between thunderous seizures of music. Melancholy Mr Swithin, he lived for religious abandonment and for conducting his sopranos. They broke his heart – which explained the twitch on him; and on all of us at practice.

Evensong was purgatory. I was opting out.

On the third Sunday in September, I left our house at six o'clock as usual to walk up Longbridge Lane to Calvary. I stopped by Windeatt's for some Polo mints and then, bowels stirring with mischievousness, I ducked behind some oak trees on a patch of grassland across from St. John's.

Waiting and watching in darkness. The odd leaf skipping by. Until evensong resurrected itself for yet another toe-curling week. If God only knew what people put themselves through in His name.

Someone should write a letter.

From between the branches, I could see manoeuvres commence: Mr Ketland – alongside a table of prayer books at the rear of the church – his head bowed but one eye lingering on his favourites among the pubescent seraphim; a barebone choir, led by Reverend Garnett, making its way through a congregation of four who had survived to another day. After a few minutes, I hurried across Longbridge Lane to the church's side door, past the choir vestiary on the right and into the men's washroom.

There they were. Apostles. Three of them, all flush for the reaping.

It took seconds. Spare coins, cigarettes and, the previous Sunday, a wallet with fifty quid. Overcoats in a welcoming row.

Clearing out the third set of pockets, I heard a distant squeak. St. John's shoe?

I rushed to the urinal and desperately tried to slash into fragrant porcelain.

The washroom door eased open. In walked Mr Ketland, the whey-faced, straitened Welshman – anywhere between thirty and sixty – with a curt manner and polished brogues. Recently promoted from Austin gear-cutter to foreman, he was therefore newly converted to Tory politics as well as spiritual rigour. And neckties. The factory-worker menopause like no other. He stood and observed me as a hysterectomy might the immaculate conception.

'Evening, Mr Ketland,' I said. 'Damp night.'

Hands in pockets, he sought guidance. How do you supervise a parish lavatory, O Lord?

I yawned. He had likely noticed my three absences from evensong. Had Ma been informed? Reverend Garnett? I'd never considered that last week's harvest might have led to *complaints* and *investigations*.

My ears felt hot.

'Arrived late for choir,' I told him, shaking my dick of nonexistent pee. 'Better get off home.'

Mr Ketland was looking fierce. I was in for it. On top of the Blanchland House fuss. It would be jail next: Wormwood Scrubs – skinned alive. Maybe I should invite Mr Ketland to the catechism group.

Desperate measures, Enoch.

Instead of slipping the cock back into its jeans, I let it flop out, turning around slowly so that he could see my uncut length. He stared at it, his chest rising and falling beneath the phony regimental tie.

I spat into my fingers and began massaging the head like I was soaping in a bathtub. With fingers and thumb I pulled the foreskin back and forth: see it stretch and have a nice day. Happy teatime marshmallow rising from the flames, Mr Ketland?

I offered him a lick.

He murmured something unforeman-like and walked towards me, breathing rapidly.

Hit me or fuck, I thought, patting the shaft of my dick left and right.

As he approached, I reached deftly for his groin and there, beneath his neatly pressed twill trousers, lay the stiffness of redemption.

Slipping his cock out from beneath layers of flannel, I began jacking him.

'You're bad news, Enoch Jones,' he said hoarsely, pulling me against his Norfolk jacket. He smelled of Old Spice.

'Aren't I,' I replied, adjusting my grip.

He knelt down heavily and sucked for a minute or two as I rested my hand on his Brylcreemed head.

Eventually he struggled back to his feet. 'Sooner you're in reform school, the better for us all.'

'First line of a hymn, Mr Ketland?'

He started kissing me on the lips. I felt sick to my socks but liked the taste of skin. Even his. How did he know about Blanchland House?

'Minute you and that Vera Jones walked into St. John's ...' he began, throat straining, '... ugly customers.'

I yanked the Austin prick harder and harder.

He buried his face in my shoulder.

'Oh, Jesus,' he moaned, thrusting for eternity and God himself. Almost there.

'Jesus, yeah,' I whispered catechismistically, steadying myself against the urinal.

'Pair of you,' he gasped, beginning a lengthy choking sound as he reached for my ass, 'not from around here ...'

'That's it, man.'

'Trash,' he managed to say, quivering from base to apex.

And he came – or rather, sputtered – over my anorak sleeve.

'You were right then, Mr Ketland,' I said, squirting jism onto the tiled floor. Something simultaneous to remember me by.

'Caravan runts,' he said, still gripping my elbow.

'Yeah,' I agreed, fastening my jeans. 'Not your sort at all.'

'Next time you'll be reported,' he added, zipping up and checking himself in the mirror.

'For bringing you off, like?' I replied, hurrying towards the line of coats.

'You know what for,' he said, turning off a tap. With wet hands, straightening his tie.

'Brilliant, Mr Ketland.'

'Hop it or I'll change my mind, lad.'

Before you could say Jack Robinson I was out on Turves Green, taking the back route home by the Carisbrooke flats so I wouldn't bump into Ma on Longbridge Lane. She of a Sunday night. Imbued with holy spirit, serenading the pub for a wee dram more.

Loose change and cigarettes in my pocket. 'God, I love evensong!' I yelled out loud. Benediction felt sticky in my Y-fronts as I started to catch on. Ma, Graham and me, we really weren't from around here. It showed. Trailer trash: love 'em, fuck 'em, or hate 'em; it's all the same.

Christ, I'm dim.

It's truly eye-opening when you're in communion with everything you're not supposed to see. Maybe my family was not so out of the ordinary, keeping everything that mattered under wraps. We'd fit right in if the locals let us. Still, it isn't pretty when grown-ups – well, mother and fathers and church warden, so far – will do anything to keep you in shadow, fingers and thumbs in front of your face.

But I had Mr Ketland to thank for letting me see beneath a pair of Longbridge trousers. The way you discover things about yourself – trash? bog whore? nancy-boy? – is when you're not expecting to. Even the worst sounding places – and people – can turn you right around.

If I'd had a breakthrough that autumn Sunday night, it was downright confusing. Nothing seemed to mesh except for one small thing: the taste of someone's mouth, the solid heft of him in my hand. The way it ended with you back on the street; and from something like happiness, wanting to call out to sleeping houses.

Word made flesh.

No St. Paul, me, but finally, at one of St. John's blessed services – albeit in the wrong room – I'd had a fearful glimpse of heaven.

At seventeen, more than most would wish to see.

I was growing more optimistic about reform school.

IN THE TIME OF SILLY PUDDING

The reason Mike Malin was not locked up in one of Her Majesty's maximum security prisons was because he was our physical training coach at Blanchland House in this remote County Durham detention centre. So inmates said. But just at my eighteenth birthday, I learned how to out-Herod Herod, as you might put it. Shut Mikey up for good; but not before I lost my own tongue through someone's else's monkey-tricks.

He was a Cockney boxer – in all he did – but his rhythm quickly, and often, faltered. Never sure of anyone. Except that he did *like* people – well, offenders. Stop-and-start Mike Malin. That's what made him scary to a lot of the blokes. You got the feeling he might one day slice your neck, then stop himself and apologize to the severed head.

Of all the staff, Mike was straightforwardly terrifying. Devoted. Friendly, even. But terrifying. Everything about him was too intense and out of focus, like someone driving through a blizzard crying. Discipline was the devil that tormented him. We all noticed it. He tried too hard.

Most of the guys made an effort to be on side. Because he was psychopathic, maybe. But also because in him we sniffed our own.

I used to watch Mike Malin on the ride to our weekly cross-country run up at Hexhamshire. The common was south of Allendale, a small town where at New Year the locals wore burning barrels on their heads. In his early thirties, husky for a gym teacher, Mike had that dartboard face of a teenage acne victim. Strawberry blond curly hair which earned him the nickname 'Giggles'. When he talked – gumdrops habitually in mouth – his eyes darted left and right as though racing cars sped in both directions. His feet waltzed about. Uppercut always at the ready. Then he'd lunge into a sentence –

torrent of some kind, well-meant usually – and retreat just as deftly.

Jab, stab, withdraw.

'You've heard the village names hereabouts, gentlemen,' he would yell above the engine of our military-green bus. 'Wolf Hills, Burnhope Seat, Black Hill, and Hangman?'

Up and down the vehicle he paced like a fighter tugging rope, saying the same thing he always said.

'Beauties, aren't they? Howle, Dye House, Eals, and Cold Fell? They're named that for a reason.'

Expecting no replies, only laughter and awe, he thrust his cratered face at each pair of us. 'The reason is we're in the *quagmire* here. Got it, boys? Vasectomized goat desert. Hundreds of miles from fucking anywhere. Miserable, bloodthirsty locals – our Sydney Roebuck the driver included – and the Scottish Menace at the border. Don't even think of striking out, lads. We use fang dogs to bring you back. They ain't polite.'

It was funny the first week.

Most fellas thought that by repeating himself, Mike was actually daring us to escape. How I read him was different: he repeated himself because he was scared of what it would mean if he didn't. Rote was his anchor.

As my release date neared, his was the seismic temperament I didn't want but was rapidly assuming: life at too full a tilt. I needed to make a home somewhere. Put the brakes on. Calm down. I needed work, friends and cash.

More than anything, I wanted to see Mike snap and recover. Or snap and fail. One way or the other. Then maybe I'd really learn a lesson.

Of anyone at Blanchland, it was Mike who would have something to impart. Although it was difficult to guess it sometimes. Take his rigmarole on these Allen Valley bus rides, for instance. Man, was he a body in trouble. We did it every Wednesday. Through the harsh landscape – scrub, gorse bushes. Moorland with nothing but Hadrian's Wall thirty miles to the north, fells all around as far as the eye could see, Newcastle-upon-Tyne to the furthest east, Carlisle to the west. In winter it *was* bleak.

Mike was right, we were in the middle of nowhere. Every one of us. 'Exact centre of the British Isles is Allendale,' he would always say as he unnecessarily scrolled down the vinyl destination 'Allendale' across from the driver. We never collected passengers, never went into Allendale. But Mike – to get everything shipshape – had his sign up.

'Oiled and greased, sailor?' he would ask the elderly man who drove us.

'Ay, ay, young cap'n!' Sidney Roebuck would reply; he knew the words by heart, too.

'Anchors h-up!' Mike would holler. Some guys bowed their heads in disbelief at his routine. Others chuckled or looked out at fields.

Blanchland's single-decker nosed its way onto the main road.

High point of seven days.

As always, Mike would instruct Mr Roebuck to park in a lay-by to the south of town near a riverside towpath.

On this frosty March morning, I kept to the last straggle of runners as usual. Head down, I was thinking over the birthday card Ma had mailed – first news I'd received in three months, 'Happy 18th. Love, Ma. (Graham has shingles.)' – and whether this was a normal key-of-the-door greeting, when I tripped, hitting my head on a boulder.

When the four or so blokes following saw that I was uninjured and about to get to my feet, they continued running. But I noticed in their faces that if I was attempting to scram, it was none of their affair.

But I couldn't budge.

'Hey! Back!' I yelled, dabbing a sticky forehead.

Crimson T-shirts and runners bobbed away through the heathery slope.

A nippy wind gusted back.

Okay, I thought. I'll shelter in these bushes, enjoy the morning off – and wait for Mike Malin.

I should have known better.

None of the boys mentioned my accident, so I later discovered. Enoch Jones's absence wasn't even noticed until roll-call, which Mike took at Blanchland House – big mistake – instead of at the roadside before boarding.

No one returned to my aid until dark. I'd even begun to miss Mike's rants. Being alone for so many hours, I realized how much I did like him. Hokey as it sounded, he felt like an older brother – or more. By dusk, I was almost weeping with the thought of Mike Malin; as though I loved the bugger. I must have been suffering from exposure. That fresh air.

On I went for hours, nose in the ferns. Mike this. Mike that. But I was opening up somehow – it felt spectacular. As police and Alsatian tracker-dogs closed in on me north from Nookton Fell over the Derwent and west from Dukesfield Fell scrambling over valleys and stepping-stones. Roadblocks at the Cowshill junction outside Catton. I faced a rude awakening.

Governor Reginald Satchell had declared an escape.

On local radio and TV news. Enoch Jones: notorious once again. Mugshot an' all, apparently. When all that time I was tits down in gorse scrub, sharing a seven-hour moment with the National Trust: gushing over the phys. ed. instructor.

Had I escaped Blanchland, I would have become a popular hero revered by most inmates: like the Great Train Robber, Ronnie Biggs. But by evening I was stretched out under blankets in the detention centre infirmary.

Overseen by a po-faced Governor Satchell determined on arrest, Mike Malin and my personal officer Alf Wreay, Nurse Crowe had examined the ankle and determined, much to Mike and Alf's evident relief, that it was sprained. I could not possibly, therefore, have been trying to abscond. She lifted strands of her hair that had fallen free and indicated that the Dirt Pot policeman could now remove my handcuffs.

Later that night, I hit the infirmary for a second time.

On my return to Blanchland, media crew at the gates – and after the medical reprieve – for nearly an hour in the gym, Mike had massaged both my legs and assisted Mrs Crowe with the ankle-bandaging before returning me to the dorm.

I knew something was wrong when I went in. The five other lags were pissed. Satchell had locked everyone down for the afternoon. No passes. No afternoon recreation. The Blanchland population had been on its bunks for hours – and wanted blood. Even the carbolic soap, rancid socks and urine seemed more pungent than usual. It didn't take long before Joe Murton and Eric Wychiffe put a few fists to their seething anger – and told me to clear out of Blanchland *like an ace*, or put up.

You don't ask why the officers are never around during these beatings. Necessary ritual, I suppose, like a good, communal rub-down. Even though you had to *bribe* staff for the blind eye to a rape. So what could I do? I let the dorm-mates – and a few others – pummel my guts and kick my head. Loser. Sag ass. I put up a defence of sorts. In the end I just curled up into a ball and took the knuckle-dusting as more crap on a pitiful day.

In the middle of the night, dreaming of underwater skeletons chattering – or shivering – their way through a sunken ship, I awoke with my leg in some kind of spasm.

'Stop,' I hushed at it. But the trotting up and down really wouldn't stop. It was like a Dr Strangelove dog. 'Stop, stop.'

Then my other leg started.

'Officer! Lad in trouble! Officer!'

Away I was carried to the infirmary past sheepish-looking room-mates. My limbs waving about like spastic umbrella spokes in a gale.

'Dr Abbotts will be here soon,' said Mrs Crowe, who had been on duty for far too long. 'Coming in from Dirt Pot.'

I closed my swollen eyes.

Someone yanked the curtain aside and in peered an elderly County Durham man with freckles and the remains of a short-back-and-sides haircut: Dr Abbotts. Behind him the usual family of Mike Malin and Nurse Crowe both with end-of-programme reports and sentence plans (I'd be leaving May 31st – already the powers-that-be were summing up my stay and 'examining inmate targets' big time). Next to Mike was Alf Wreay, the officer assigned to me at the outset, who was nodding as though I'd won the World Cup.

'Got a black eye on the moors, too, Mr Jones?' said the doctor in a mature man's knowing way. His breath smelled of cider.

Nothing like a bust-up to unite men.

'Expect so, sir.'

Saying nothing, he took a cursory look over my chest, back and legs – evidently dismissing the dorm-mates' handiwork as some kind of virile roughhousing.

To my surprise, he said, 'We'll get a few X-rays. The convulsions are a release from that massage of yours, Malin. But the lad's skull needs looking at.'

'Right you are,' replied Mike, stepping closer.

'Boy's not accustomed, I daresay.'

'No,' chortled Mike gamefully, stepping back and around with my dossier.

'Not a sporting lad, are you, Jones?'

'Yes I am, sir,' I replied, trying to fuck his diagnosis.

'To Hexham Medical Centre in the morning?' said Nurse Crowe.

Dr Abbotts yanked the curtain shut again, for some reason winking at me as he did so. Ah, lads. What golden days.

'It'd better be tonight,' he said, in a quiet but audible voice.

'I'll drive Enoch myself,' offered Mike.

'Let that governor of yours know,' said the doctor. 'No more escape stories on the wireless. Dirt Pot were in a right stir.'

Mrs Crowe tut-tutted.

'May I see Jones's file, Nurse?' continued the doctor.

Shuffling of paper and the hum of fluorescent lights. I closed my eyes, desperate for some rest. I tried to recall the afternoon on Hexhamshire Common. An escape, but not in their terms. Up there with a kestrel or two, the smell of moss and goat pellets, mile upon mile of open scree.

What I had discovered about my feelings for Mike Malin had stayed with me, as well. I wasn't ashamed. Blanchland was going to be about him, I decided. If this was a schoolgirl's crush, in the bright lights I admitted it. Call it what you will. My sexuality was like some shadow-boxer, anyway. I'd never rule out a woman. Mike was helping me back to women, maybe – but I'd kiss that madman first.

'Where's the lad's record, Nurse?' said Dr Abbotts softly. But I could hear every syllable. 'Epilepsy, seizures, that kind of thing. Family history – where's that page?'

'It's usually at the back,' said Mrs Crowe.

More sifting of papers. Clicking of a ballpoint. I was dreaming into the shipwreck again and my skeletal pals' chatter.

'I don't see any family,' grumbled Dr Abbotts.

'Oh, here we are,' said Mike, always helpful.

A chair leg scraped.

'Yes,' Mrs Crowe was saying. 'I see.'

'Lad was *adopted*,' explained the doctor. 'Says so at the top: "Teenage pregnancy".'

'No father mentioned?' asked Mike.

The room felt suspended.

'I don't think the lad….' It was Alf Wreay's voice.

'Right then,' said the doctor. 'No family history.'

Another scraping of the chair leg. Men muttering.

'The X-rays will tell us what we need,' Dr Abbotts went on cheerily, his voice trailing away out of the room. 'Not to worry!'

I glared at the ceiling pipes.

Lad was adopted?

Could they have got that wrong? It didn't sound like it. No father. Teenaged ma.

Adopted.

Nurse Crowe pulled the curtain aside and laid my clothes on the bed.

Right then, Dr Abbotts had said. Adopted is all right.

'Get dressed, Enoch,' said Mrs Crowe wearily. 'We haven't done with you yet.'

I put on my bomber jacket, trousers, and one boot.

Graham has shingles, I remembered suddenly. 'Happy 18th.

Love, Ma.' Who were these people back in Birmingham? Ma and stepfather Graham? Frank, now in Dagenham. Was he my real dad – Frank Jones? Or Vera my real mother? Or neither? Why hadn't anyone told me? Who the hell are my parents, I thought, as I sat on the bed facing the curtain? Enoch was my real name? Jones?

Could you get a straight answer? 'About my adoption, Mrs Crowe?'

'Yes, love.'

'Well …'

'It's all confidential, Enoch. Don't you worry.'

'No,' I said, trying to work out how to phrase it. 'Well … how did anyone know?'

'From your mother, I expect.'

'My mother?' I asked, realizing I now had two.

'Your adoptive mother. Vera, isn't it? She would have had to explain it on the intake form. We need family histories, you see.'

'I see.'

'Vera's health and your father's – adoptive father's that is, Frank – wouldn't be relevant.'

'Right.'

'There was no tracing of your birth mother or anything,' she said, reassuringly.

'No.'

'So the record's blank. But don't you worry. We'll get the X-rays….'

She checked the clock and sighed. It was 3 a.m.

'Okay.'

'I won't leak it to the other boys, Enoch.'

I must have looked concerned.

'No.'

'I know what they're like. Anyone who's a bit different, huh? Wham-bam, thank you, ma'am.'

'Right.'

You try to laugh along.

'I'll get you a big sock,' said Mrs Crowe.

'So it's quite definite then?'

'What is, love?' she replied, ferreting through hosiery in the First Aid cupboard and holding something to the light.

'The adoption. That I was adopted.'

She handed over a mammoth sock, and I grasped it as you might the prize-winning catch.

'Why would Vera make up a thing like that?'

I shook my head.

'You can't tell fibs on those documents, Enoch,' she added, leaning forward to help me with the stocking. 'There's some oath....'

Mrs Crowe was about to thrust my foot into the gaping woollen maw but stopped. Just like Mike Malin would do, in mid-sentence.

No shortcuts for Vera Jones on this one, then. How it must have pained her, such honesty. What a risk. On a form that I might see. Or hear.

Why hadn't she told me?

'Enoch?' said Nurse Crowe, leaving me to the sock, and putting a finger to her lips.

Gradually I eased the foot into its home. The lady stared at me in disbelief – and we looked at one another and at the coarse sock.

'No idea,' I replied, this new mother coming into view.

'What puddings,' said Mrs Crowe annoyed, returning to her desk and tidying it at a clip. 'What silly, silly puddings.'

I listened for Mike Malin's footsteps – and the promise of more hours at large, as far as Hexham and some radiation. The world raced me by. Couldn't I even feel curiosity, passion for a guy without the ground opening up beneath me? First, Alsatian dogs on a common. Now the rewritten history and a family of lies. But motherland, paternity – they would have to wait. First, it'd be Mike.

'Oiled and greased, sailor?' he said, appearing at the door, waving a security night-clearance like a farewell glove.

'Anchors h-up' was what he expected. Goofy prick, was what I felt.

So I told him, 'I love you, Mike.' Getting to the point.

It was more emotion than I had ever expressed.

Like a stalled ox, Mike dithered between the entrance and Nurse Crowe's chair. Maybe it was more feeling than he'd ever heard – because he never spoke to me again.

Mrs Crowe did say this was the time of silly puddings: mothers out of a hat, punch-ups and an afternoon with kestrels and the odd goat. I was another Dr Abbotts, with a tongue gone ape-shit, I guess. Letting out a secret; on the lam before due date.

But now my past was far sillier than a pudding. It stood in the centre of a room, not unlike Mike Malin – raw, petrified, its mouth ajar like a sock-in-waiting. What would that say about love, I wondered? Or origins?

When you look them in the face – and there's not a sound.

THE BOMBMAKER

Bombings. Strikes. Prime Minister Edward Heath declares State of
Emergency. – *The London Times*, November 13, 1973

Hundreds of birds in the air
And millions of leaves on the pavement
   – Sir John Betjeman, Poet Laureate,
      on the marriage of HRH Princess Anne to Capt. Mark Phillips,
     November 14, 1973

Nibbling toast, Major Chubb sat there with his harelip stuck in the
Times. Grumbling something – 'Procession of the Garter', it sounded
like. 'Henley …' As though listing dates on a calendar. 'Ascot Week,
Glyndebourne …' It was my first breakfast at Sassoon Lodge, his
government-approved 'transition home' in Brighton. June 1, 1973.
'Trooping the Colour. Derby Day …'

    I'd turned eighteen up north in a male detention centre called
Blanchland. The six-month sentence (burglary) – courtesy of a
Birmingham magistrate, Mrs Lennox – involved a final year here on
the south coast of England and gradual re-entry into civilization.
This was the finishing-school period of my life which put me off
Britain and detention for good.

    If only Mrs Lennox had known what Chubbsy gave us to read
every night. First World War versifier Siegfried demented Sassoon!
Diaries. Poems! Yet somehow I couldn't forget the volumes Major
Chubb placed by our beds, a voice from Flanders trenches.

    Casement wide open, over toast and Darjeeling you could smell
the seaweed from the Major's halfway house; choked-up, Edwardian
living room near Old Steine, a fishermen's neighbourhood. What

sticks with me too, though – and I can't figure it – is the corner of his newspaper hanging into a fancy china teacup.

Ignored, I was taking a boo at the page facing me across the table – there was one dandy of an advertisement. I thought at first it was a joke: 'Lost, adored Grey London Pigeon. Known as "birdy". Not ringed.' Or a secret message?

The two other 'guests' – that's what Major Chubb calls us – Jeanie Williams and Randy Crumm, sixteen, work at the seafront Grand Hotel. Chambermaid and bellhop. Randy hints at sparetime bombmaking. But he's mainly a bum boy – cash only. Pair of teenaged softies, this particular morning they weren't saying owt, just scooping up scrambled eggs and ketchup, sneaking an odd look at me – fresh meat from reform school, northeast England moors.

I am bound to get it in the neck sometime…. And death is the best adventure of all – better than living in idleness and sinking into the groove again and trying to be happy.

– Siegfried Sassoon, *Diary*, April 4, 1916

Major Chubb was supposed to be interviewing me – a kind of orientation session – like Governor Satchell did at Blanchland House up at Allendale. But 'top of the pops', as Jeanie calls him, just kept on gnawing. Veins over his cheekbones slithering like seams.

I made out more of his backpage birdy: 'Flew off from Hingham, Norfolk, 7 p.m. Saturday 26 May, 1973. Would be homing towards London. Could easily fly into house looking for food. Please keep, and contact Amanda Fielding. 01 352 3224.'

Homing. A lost homer? This Amanda was for real.

Jeanie was in cheap denims and an orange, hand-knitted jersey. I stared at her little tits. Girls. All the time at Blanchland we talked about shagging bitch; then we'd use each other.

Chomp, chomp, chomp goes the Major, plump and smelling of men's cologne. Dress shoes and pullover. Shirt, tie. I kind of liked his interviewing style. And Jeanie's little tits.

SECRETARY OF STATE, HOME OFFICE, WHITEHALL

H.M. DETENTION CENTRES (BLANCHLAND HOUSE)

REGULATIONS

– RECEPTION AND REMOVAL –

(i) Reception:

Search –

8. – (1) Every inmate shall be searched by an officer on reception at a Centre, and at such subsequent times as may be directed, all unauthorized articles taken from him.

– (2) The searching of an inmate shall be conducted in as seemly a manner as is consistent with the necessity of discovering any concealed article.

Eight months at Blanchland had turned me upside down: all those cross-country runs, physical training, hand-jobs in the shower block, kit inspections, parade at dawn, margarine fuck-ins at the outhouse farm. On the double, lads. Break a ball. No visits from Ma or Graham Dagg, nor a peep from the old man Frank. Card on my birthday. Nowt else. Suited me.

Couldn't get girls – or humping generally – off my mind. Not just goers like our skinny Jeanie. Gonna bang her before I'm finished, I resolved over breakfast, day one. But she'd be the half of it.

I stared and stared at the back of Chubbsy's page. It makes you want to give up. Amanda Fielding has taken out a three-inch *bordered* advertisement in a national newspaper to track down a stray pigeon. Bold print. A grey London pigeon. Do I want to live in a country like this?

Thank you, sir.

I picture Amanda Fielding's pigeon as a young, spirited female – someone like the Canadian prime minister's wife who was now turned towards me on page three of the *Times* – striding through a park to some Commonwealth Day service in Westminster Abbey. Looking a bit far from home, sleeves too long. White, snow white.

How you wanted to follow her. Shoes too new. Grey rosy-cheeked. Walking stiff in packed-to-the-gills London. But she could fly.

Home, as Amanda would say.

'Faster, Jones.' Mattress shop, change clothes. Kitchen work, garden, change clothes again. Shower. Carpentry, mailbags. 'Two towels, Jones? On report.' But Mr Malin, sir. Blunt razors. No slacking. Run, run, run. Keys at warders' thighs, like breaking glass. Cut your way out. Reminders, reminders. No sir. Yes, Mr Wreay. Never, sir. Yes, sir. Right away. Scrub floors, sweep, mop. Only a lot of yelling, Enoch. Jump to it. Smell of acrid soap, piss and bodies. Hundred youths. Clip around the ear. Dwarves, devils. Do I love you, Mike Malin? Can't last long, can't last long.

The bullet and the bayonet are brother and sister. If you don't kill him, he'll kill you. Stick him between the eyes, in the throat, in the chest or round the thighs. If he's on the run, there's only one place; get your bayonet into his kidneys; it'll go in as easy as butter. Don't waste good steel. Six inches are enough – what's the use of a foot of steel sticking out of the back of a man's neck? Three inches will do him, and when he coughs, go and find another.

– Siegfried Sassoon, *Diary*, April 25, 1916

Don't worry, Mrs Trudeau. There will always be an Amanda Fielding from Norfolk. We all know *her* problem, if you know what I mean. England's an animal kingdom, no matter where you home. Just don't tell Amanda you're a dope-toking free spirit under that Big Charcoal Hat, will you? She might withdraw her ad. Then where would we be? Unwanted, unringed pigeons, length and breadth of the isles.

'Passing bread, Jones? On report. Lose all privileges.' Thank you, sir. Bunk inspection, drill and slophouse. 'Skip to it, sonny boy.'

I'd have been better off as Margaret Trudeau or a pigeon's length, someone classified. Badge of courage, as the screws call it, dripping from my hunkers. Perched on a telegraph wire. Poised.

'*Mary Poppins, War and Peace, Godspell* or *Bridge on the River Kwai*, Jones?' said Major Chubb suddenly, from behind his paper. Tea rising up the back page like bird poop across a ceiling. I wasn't sure what he meant. Jeanie and Randy were mouthing something I couldn't make out.

'*Mary Poppins* it is then,' he said, carefully folding the newspaper and rising to shake my hand. 'Good work, men.'

He left. Interview over.

H.M. DETENTION CENTRES (BLANCHLAND HOUSE)
OFFICER'S REPORT – PRIOR TO DISCHARGE

NAME: ENOCH JONES NUMBER: 5678345
OFFICER: WREAY

1. DOES HE OBEY QUICKLY AND WILLINGLY?
2. IS HE RESPONSIVE?
3. DOES HE DISPLAY MAXIMUM EFFORT ALL THE TIME?
4. IS HE RESPECTFUL AND CO-OPERATIVE?

Three months later, Randy Crumm started to get on my wick.

Every second Saturday evening – between five and ten (before our weekend curfew) – was a private, completely illegal 'Naked Night' at the Briars, a fag guesthouse off Cannon Place. One of Randy's haunts, full of rich, sissy London punters.

It was September and we were into an Indian summer, as the Major called it: seven airless, sticky days and nights. I was getting antsy so I went along with Randy. 'Gotta put yourself about a bit, Enoch,' he told me after we'd stripped down at the cloakroom and walked into the saloon. We must have been the youngest there. Randy was underage, anyway. 'Look at Her Majesty,' he said, oblivious to the stares we were getting. 'In Canada this summer with the Duke of Edinburgh.' I nodded and sat next to him at the bar. 'Keeping the Commonwealth together. Now they're off somewhere else. You gotta keep busy, mate. Lizzy Two ain't knitting socks all day.'

Randy's stranger than Amanda Fielding. He gets all this regal shit from Major Chubb. It's so infectious, bigwig baloney, the kid actually thinks he's part of the play.

Once I watched a scattering of gulls that followed the newly-turned furrows; their harsh wrangle mingling with the faint creak and rattle of the plough, as they swung and settled like enormous grey snow-flakes. While the team halted at the hedge, and the man was turning, with a grumble at the wretchedness of the day, they all sat like some cloaked, attentive congregation, yet their bills were busy at the soil: then the big steady horses moved forward again, with a confusion of dull-silvery wings flickering in the wake of the toilers, as the queer procession began another journey across the stubble.

– Siegfried Sassoon, *Diary*, January 23, 1917

I tried not to look but Randy was hung like a mule; some black and purple 'Love' tattoo – with mermaids – sprawled down his groin.

'Princess Anne's in Kiev. They get around, the royals. Ted Heath the prime minister rushed all the way back from that Ottawa conference to come in fifty-first in the Admirals Cup.'

'Busy week,' I replied, aware of a room full of bare bodies, every age and shape, knocking back beer.

'Morning Cloud's his boat. Gotta get about, Enoch. Two pints of bitter, Jack. Or you go flat on your bazookas.'

So I was a shut-away. Was that Randy's point? I met enough docile tourists at the Pavilion to keep me going for years. A part-time guide job the Major had found in addition to my place at Brighton's sixth-form college: two A levels and a course in personal hygiene.

Royal families, what donkey's asses: George iv, who built the palace I work in, was a classic. He was Prince of Wales and Prince Regent when he built Brighton's Pavilion, waiting to take over the kingdom from his dad. People called him 'Prinny' – dad-hater – and he was keen on style. Arabian Nights; a massive, onion-turd building in the middle of an English 'taking-the-cure' seaside town. Complete oddity. Turban roof, wonky windows and Taj Mahal towers. That's how angry he was at his dad. 'Prinny' was the guy who fell in love with a giraffe, remember – a camelopard, he called it.

Yet people worry about the likes of me!

Randy believed in these people. Kings, queens, princes and prime ministers. He even sounded like the Major some days. Kid had been in Brighton and Sassoon Lodge for too many months: swallowing everything Chubbsy told him, hook, line and sinker. So I was surprised when Randy spilled the beans about his little bombmaking hobby, in a effort to recruit me, and his plan for the autumn Conservative Party Conference at the Grand Hotel. A sign he wasn't completely taken in, I suppose.

At Briars Guesthouse there were thirty or so men – and only men – in the saloon. Even its two landlords were starkers, cockproud leaning over the counter. I was surprised at how natural everyone seemed. Birmingham was never like this. I pretended to listen to Randy. Another of his weirdnesses was Richard Nixon impersonations. The American president was in the news a lot because he wouldn't hand over the tapes, which drove Randy bananas. In retaliation for the Yank's obstinacy, he'd memorized some of Nixon's speeches. On Palace Pier or at breakfast at Sassoon Lodge, Randy'd launch into a tirade. Sometimes it was hilarious – clever even, for a sociopath.

Maybe Naked Night made Randy nervous. Or *I* did. We'd fallen quiet, so off he went like he was on U.S. television: 'I pledge to you tonight, my fellow Americans and Enoch our novice, that I will do all I can to ensure that one of the results of Watergate is a new level of political decency and integrity in America,' at which point he slammed his hand on a table mat and burst into laughter. Not everyone knew how to take it. But the wrinkly old-timers next to us chuckled, ordering beer all round.

Later, we walked to the dimly lit terrace out back. More bodies gathered in groups or strolling solo under the trellises. I knew there was action; it was a poofter hangout, after all. I also knew Randy turned tricks for a fiver. How else could he amass so much money in his room? The Major deposited all our 'legal' earnings in a trust account for when we 'graduated'. Randy's stash was limp-loot: married men and pensionable fairies.

Three or so men were jacking each other off. You sauntered past, under the coloured lights, glad they were having such a hot time. I wondered if Randy really was queer or just getting about, as he says.

I couldn't work him out. He and Jeanie were pretty tight – even if they had arguments, like today. Randy hesitated, then leaned against the wall. Looking quite different now, he seemed afraid.

'Suck me, Enoch,' he said.

Today we march eleven miles back to Morlancourt. Molyneux (my servant) was very communicative last night; his tongue was slightly loosened by beer ... He told me he loved me like a brother – very nice of him; he *is* a dear.

– Siegfried Sassoon, *Diary*, June 26, 1916

'Not into it,' I said, leaning against the wall. I *knew* the guy! Crazy as he was, I liked him. Two fellas were nuzzling in on another man's armpits. I tried to look distracted.

'The notes,' said Randy. 'You've been in my room again.'

Again? His bomb-making notes: four typewritten pages, dangerous in the wrong hands.

'You wouldn't want Chubbsy to know,' he added. 'Stealing's a crime.'

'I didn't take anything.'

'Suck or I talk.' He slapped his hard-on against my leg; grabbed my shoulder.

'Talk to who, Randy?'

'Wanna go back to Blanchland House?'

'Why would I nick something like that?'

' 'Cos you're a criminal, Enoch.'

He grabbed my cropped head and pushed. I could smell the chip shop on him. Cheesy and sour. But I worked him over good. Randy started necking with one of the blokes next to us. Maybe he is a sagarse. Who knows. Or maybe it's just like Blanchland: no bloody choice; your accuser a judge and jury. Besides, I did steal his sheaf of notes. I'd got the feeling he meant business with his explosives recipe. Someone was mailing the stuff to him. The British authorities aren't very nice to bombers. Even when it's Tories shot to pieces in the sky. I was doing him a favour. Big brotherly. At Black Rock swimming pool, I'd thrown the lot over a fence into the English Channel.

Two mud-stained hands were sticking out of the wet ashen chalky soil, like the roots of a shrub turned upside down. They might have been imploring aid; they might have been groping and struggling for life and release: but the dead man was hidden; he was buried; his hideous corpse was screened from the shame of those who lay near him, their agony crying out to heaven.

– Siegfried Sassoon, *Diary*, April 22, 1917

At 'Prinny's' Brighton Pavilion, I don't say much to the tourists. I can't. I'd piss myself. Every now and again I answer some North American or Japanese stupidity along with all the British thickness I face. People'll believe anything if it's packaged right. I make it up, half the time, say it's Regency, baroque, romantic, rococo, *picturesque*. Anything to gloss over some awkward Polaroid-led 'question and answer' bout. Admirers of British history are a clueless bunch. It's British civility that attracts the overseas brigade. Shame at their home country's thin culture, longing for stabilities and ancestry they'll never have. I'm ever so *civil*; especially as I'm trying to get tips as well as an education.

Then I aim the Anglophiles at our Yellow Drawing Room where they ooh and aah at Fum and Hum, the Two Birds of Royalty. Oriental peacocks painted on the wall. I wonder what Amanda Fielding would say about that? All the way from Hingham. After the Music Room they shuffle to a Banqueting Room where, for as long as their necks can take it, they gaze up at the Flying Dragon Gasolier.

I talk about the FDG at great length – and in minute detail, describing one dragonly feature after another – seeing how long the tourist head will endure. If only the lamp'd burst into flames for once. Fum and Hum with North Sea energy shooting out of their eyes and arses. I don't tell visitors that 'Prinny' actually spent most of his time in the kitchen downstairs because he preferred simplicity. Or that he was in love with a giraffe. I tried honesty once. People started grimacing, turning away to other *objets d'art* and their fantasies. Next day my boss got a letter complaining about the 'docent' (me) and 'falling standards' (mine). I lost a day's pay.

After the (censored) tour, I stand by a portico holding out my hand: a penny for the Commonwealth, loss of Empire, Margaret Thatcher's campaign for prime minister, Royal Doulton china, Royal Mint, Royal Wedding in November. Whatever. Royal Society for the Prevention of Cruelty to Animals. Royal Scotsman. Royal bog roll. Anything to get the idiots out.

Letter bombs are easier. You need thermite first. Crush some rust and heat it red in a cast-iron pot. Mix it with aluminium bits, three parts to one....

Randy's ribs flickered above me. I gagged and spat into the shrubbery. Kneeling at his feet I looked up while he was still at an armpit of the fella next to him. It must have looked kind of religious. Sacred. Randy didn't seem to notice he'd come. Like Blanchland House once more: solemn, get-it-over-with spasm. But no lock-up or army rules afterwards, not the same kind, anyway. On Saturdays we still had till 10 p.m. Normally, I'd go see a film.

'Let's get another pint,' he said, pulling away from temptation in the garden. Another tour of duty finished; tell all the recruits it never happened. I looked around at the Briars' love-terrace, wiped my hand on some ivy. 'See the stars?' Randy sang out, as we ducked under some bushes toward the light and man-chatter inside. 'Now tell me, Jones,' he said in the Major's plummiest accent, *'Battle for the Planet of the Apes, Last Tango in Paris, O Lucky Man,* or *No Sex Please, We're British?'*

He was pointing between my eyes.

'Mary Poppins it is then,' he declared. 'My notes back by Monday or I squeal, Mr Jones.'

If only they would speak out and throw their medals in the faces of their masters; and ask their women why it thrills them to know that they, the dauntless warriors, have shed the blood of Germans. Do not the women gloat secretly over the wounds of their lovers? Is there anything inwardly noble in savage sex instincts?

– Siegfried Sassoon, *Diary*, June 19, 1917

By October, Sassoon Lodge was in deep trouble. It didn't take long
before ten officers with a search warrant tore up the shelves, cupboards and floorboards, every last crease of Major Chubb's halfway
sanctuary; and spent hours questioning us.

'We're not Irish!' thundered Chubbsy up his stairs. 'It's the IRA
you want, not hardworking patriots!'

I'd never squealed on Randy; nor he on me.

The police couldn't nail us with anything. Besides, it's not illegal
for a former crook like Randy to work at Brighton's Grand Hotel.
But according to 'intelligence', reported in the *Times*, the hotel was
the focus of a possible terrorist attack. Chubbsy got a personal repri-
mand from the Home Secretary for 'allowing us to fall under suspi-
cion'! You wondered what the fuss was about, really. Did they treat
all Grand Hotel staff like this? Until a few days after the house
search; police uncovered a plot to bomb the Conservative Party
annual conference at month's end.

Randy Crumm? What a joke.

The bomb squad had discovered explosives in one of the Grand's
maintenance cupboards – adjacent to Luxury Suite 39 – which
fuelled ideas that closet-case, Tory Prime Minister Edward Heath
was an assassination target. As instructed by the Home Office, Major
Chubb wasted no time in fixing Randy – suspected bomb-making
accomplice – by arranging a transfer to his Edinburgh counterpart,
Brigadier Mackenzie, a former Sandhurst-turned-mercenary-com-
mando, known for his devastating transformation of reluctant young
offenders.

Randy would leave right after November's Royal Wedding, provided no bomb went off in Brighton. But Randy was non-bomberly
to a T: Edward Heath and the Tories enjoyed their right-wing conference; the Major, Enoch, Randy and Jeanie, we took the trip to London for Princess Anne's wedding to Mark Phillips: Dark Ages re-
enactment for the masses. But Randy hadn't finished with me yet.
Not after I confessed about stealing his notes.

Harder, sir. Harder. Sir. Thank you.

By early November, royal wedding preparations were at fever pitch. On television, three men with vacuum cleaners walked hurriedly up and down Westminster Abbey – 'from the sacrarium steps to the west door,' the journalist said. Sapphire-blue carpets unfurled, trains without their bride, over the ancient, underfloor human remains. Three men in dress shirts hoovering like no tomorrow. In the outer aisles more blokes, with mighty, pterodactyl sweepers. It was funny to imagine them preparing for Randy who, after the ceremony, would be heading to a Scottish honeymoon with Brigadier Mackenzie, the be-kilted one who'd show Randy his terms.

Early the following morning in London, Major Chubb found a precise spot in Parliament Square where Randy's Edinburgh escort was to meet us. Five hours before anything was supposed to happen, you could barely see the road for people. A young couple – Union Jack shirts and top hats – had this Danzig radio broadcasting a 'Royal Wedding Special.' I was glancing at Jeanie and Randy – who seemed thrilled at our happy-family's day out – when Larry the Raven emerged from the airwaves.

As the Major's broken blood vessels nodded out the sights: Big Ben, Houses of Parliament, and the new statue of Winston Churchill – 'Giant of a statesman. Giant. Dominating his fellow man' – I tuned in to a coastguard being interviewed about a raven. How was it I kept hearing about birds? Next it'll be Amanda Fielding on her own phone-in. What is it with the English? Pigeons, ravens, ceremonies every which way, poncing around in crowns and robes. I couldn't give a tinker's cuss. Suddenly, it was one of the Queen's yeomen – Warder J. Wilmington – on the radio talk show with the coastguard. Fuck. Yeoman Wilmington was the Tower of London's *raven master!* The Tower of London has a raven master who takes in ravens who've been stuck in cliffs!

Get a nice padded envelope with double layers from W. H. Smith. Thermite goes in the main bit with the letter. Magnesium powder in the outer layer. An explosive fuse is next.... Lay it like a baby on top of the powdered magnesium.... *Voilà*. A love letter. (If it doesn't blow up, it'll burn the shit out of a letter-opener's flesh).

The crowds further along Whitehall began cheering. Her Royal Highness and Captain Mark Phillips were supposedly on their way, but it was too difficult to see. 'Queen's Household Cavalry,' someone cried out as though he'd sighted land. But still nothing but backs of heads.

'Long drive ahead of us, Major Chubb,' repeated the Edinburgh commando for Randy, growing testy at the delayed royal display; and Chubbsy's reluctance to hand the kid over. The young couple next to us bundled their radio away, and began whooping. Major Chubb noticed the time. The convoy was very late. Impatient, the Brigadier Scot picked up Randy's kitbag and indicated they should depart. 'There's more on the telly, lad.' Randy nodded, said a hurried goodbye to Jeanie and me, shook Chubbsy's hand and that was that.

As the cries increased all around, I stared ahead at people's necks, at collars flecked in Union Jack red and blue. Jostling with the crowd, we each stood on tiptoe to see something. Anything. But there were so many flags, arms and heads. You didn't catch much. In the pandemonium, I felt a tug on my shoulder but didn't turn around. Another tug. And another.

It was Randy, tears flooding down his cheeks.

Muttering something I couldn't hear, he planted a kiss fair and square on my mouth before hurrying off through the faces again. Union Jacks. As the shouting and whistling rose to fever pitch, people elbowed to see, and I did get a glimpse – like the frame in a movie – of pale skin and jewels. Then the blackness of the road again, sound of hooves, carriage wheels, soldiers' boots.

Was I unnerved by Randy? It was like holding a Brighton pebble in my fist. Right off the beach. Unfathomable. I've got a rock in my hand right now, I thought. Uncontainable. But what was it, this feeling? A prince built the Pavilion on emotion, painted birds into walls, in a fever at his dad. So do I throw this rock high above the marchers, in celebration? Rage? Amanda's Birdy on a joyride? Or fling it down with the leaves in this gutter?

In the morning papers all week, on television and radio: 'Bombings. Strikes. Prime Minister declares a State of Emergency.' Those were the headlines staring across at us from Chubbsy's *Times* above Darjeeling and toast. England was at a standstill. Two IRA car bombings at the Home Office, another at the Hilton Hotel, three more in London's West End. Energy crisis. Power cuts. Millions of homes blacked out due to cold weather. Go-slow on the railways. Talk of rationing. Mass unemployment. Miners refusing overtime. More demonstrations.

Where have I been? Lost in Brighton Pavilion, under Major Chubbs's nose, up Jeanie, at royal weddings, in Siegfried's diaries and on the end of Randy's dick. You bring in the army when questions fly, when feelings go off like thermite. Blanchland, Mike Malin had lit the fuse.

If England was waking up at last, so was I.

Whoever needed notes, Randy Crumm?

FIRST STEPS FIRST

To hell with going back.

Nineteen and out of England for the first time, Enoch Jones had made up his mind to do a bunk. Richest move of his life. The longer he stayed with this jinxed and disgruntled band of British holiday-makers, the opportunities for disappearance increased no end. What a doomed journey for these Mediterranean-seeking three hundred. Now stranded in Madrid.

Enoch leaned against a windowpane out of the sun, when a bearded Spaniard who smelled of lemons – Borja he said his name was – immediately set upon a conversation about staircases: Blenheim Palace, Chatsworth House. The bespectacled man had stepped on the lot. Bodiam, 'the most fairy of English castles' as he put it, with its famous spiral. Another dreary Anglophile, fresh from the English makeover.

With one ear attuned to this chatty man and the other to announcements of delays and itinerary-changes that had long since got the better of the crowd, Enoch plotted his escape from Conquerors Holidays' 'air only'. The stairs-I-have-known raconteur did go on a bit: Sissinghurst's tower steps, those tricky Chartwell ones. He must be a Catholic in crisis, thought Enoch. The idea of pilgrimage – the up and down kind, on your knees preferably – appeals to that sort.

There was little for Enoch to plan: he knew no one in Spain, knew nothing about his purported destination, and had money enough only for one night, two at best. The courier arrangement being that he return to London the following evening, after delivery of a suitcase chock-a-block with architectural designs, scaled models and a ream of meticulously drafted documents in black and turquoise ink.

It crossed Enoch's mind that he was being irresponsible, maybe even breaking down. But he had nothing to lose. Certainly he felt no loyalty to Major Chubb at the Brighton 'transition home', or to the Major's entrepreneur crony Riaz Mansour from London's East End where Enoch now worked as a car park attendant – employment arranged by Chubbsy 'until something more *you* comes along'. Riaz's pipe dream – financed in large degree by the gullible Major at Sassoon Lodge – was the establishing of a 'gourmet, *à la carte* fish-and-chip shop around the swimming pool' of one of his mate's hotels, Flamingo Palace, at the teeming resort of Benidorm. Short drive from Alicante airport on the Costa Blanca. 'Great future in this for you and us,' Mr Mansour had boasted to Enoch and Chubbsy. 'We could start a chain.'

Not me.

At Madrid airport, with liberty at hand, Enoch felt even less persuaded to carry out his instructions. In fact, the unlikelihood of any personal success after going missing – and abandoning the suitcase – whetted his appetite all the more. If I don't do it now, I'll grow up like a Borja, gabbing to young Englishmen about staircases. Or something equally asinine. Checking parking permits in the rain outside a Cable Street music studio in Limehouse, East London. Or serving cod and 'french fries' in Andalucía to overweight redflesh from northern Europe.

It was early August 1974 and the two travellers – or at least one of them – engaged in staircases were part of Conquerors' jostling troupe of passengers; a very ugly concoction of hot, much-tormented charter tourists recently arrived from Heathrow and a scattering of highly apprehensive locals. All on blistering tarmac, waiting to board an Iberia shuttle bus to the plane.

'Franco! Look!' shouted a Spanish boy pulling at his mother's arm, 'Generalísimo Franco!'

One or two of *the overheated* looked in the child's direction, but most of the English were more concerned about securing seats – or more correctly, beer – on the flight ahead than paying heed to a youngster.

Already forming in the stifling air of high summer were many versions of complaint to Conquerors Holidays, who had promised their customers a direct flight to the Mediterranean port of Alicante 'with a speedy transfer to Benidorm – and your sun-filled paradise'. Not an unearthing in Spain's landlocked capital. The company representative, whose breathing now resembled contractions, was trying to inform the crowd that they would soon be 'popping over' to Barcelona on a regular scheduled flight. There, a brand-new Conquerors jet would be standing by to 'toddle on south' to Alicante.

'Ay, but will *this* bleeder make it?' said one middle-aged tourist in neat, green soccer shorts.

Miss Conquerors Representative managed to see the humour.

'We didn't vote in Harold Wilson to be treated like this, young lady,' said another, referring to Britain's new Labour prime minister and a glorious road ahead for the downtrodden; and those in transit.

The little Spanish boy, now jumping about, had his sights on the airport's cargo area.

'We want! We want!' began a burly Scot trying to recreate the mood of February's ban on miners' overtime that had led to a national strike in the United Kingdom.

'*Guapo*, no,' scolded the Spanish boy's mother – no, dear – looking around nervously at the rioting English and their embittered alien tongues. 'El Caudillo's in hospital,' she told him. Spain's elderly dictator, Francisco Franco, recovering erratically from a grave illness.

There was no stopping the boy. He had spotted Franco.

'Money back! Money back!' The chant hit a revolutionary stride, with the Scotsman's refrain of 'Lousy bunch of assoles'.

Suddenly, a fleet of eight military vehicles emerged from behind the collection of hangars. A sprightly escort across the main runway.

'*Dios mío!*' declared the boy's mother – my God! – clutching her son. 'Get down from there, Paco.'

Two or three Spaniards nudged one another and strained to see over the heads of these boisterous foreigners. 'Franco,' they were saying to one another. '*El Pardo*.' His palace. Recuperation. Dying.

Towards the rear of the procession was an old-fashioned, black

Mercedes displaying on its roof the blood-and-sun stripes of the Spanish flag – unmistakably, judging by the awestruck faces in the crowd, this *was* the Fascist leader's personal limousine.

'We want! Money back!' The Anglo-Saxon lament continued.

But the British protesters sensed attention falling away. This never happened to soccer fans abroad. What could be going on?

Tongues tied.

In the middle of this convoy was some sort of pyramid. A missile launcher perhaps. Or glittering robot. Enoch couldn't make it out so far away in the sunlight.

Chanting petered out.

Groups of spectators appeared at departure windows as the vehicles drew closer. Several Conquerors ran back inside the terminal. Spain's army, too close for comfort.

'Fuck you! Fuck you!' the burly Scot droned on in his cups, punching at the air triumphantly, but now the sole protester. 'Up yours! Bunch of assoles!'

Clearly the armed escort was an event. Observers of this unannounced march-past by their ailing general fell into a deep, if not completely respectful, hush.

'Lighten up, Eric!' One of the Scotsman's Cockney mates tapped him on the shoulder, squinting at Barajas's runway. 'Queen Mum's comin' wiv us. Look, man!'

Eric swayed to the perpendicular.

'Peasant butcher,' whispered Borja at Enoch's side, hastily replacing his sunglasses with spectacles.

'Who is?' said Enoch.

'There's a saying about men like him from Galicia.'

'General Franco?'

The man nodded wearily. 'If you meet a *gallego* on the stairs, you never know if he's going up or down.'

Enoch shaded his eyes to get a better view of the approaching vehicles. 'In the Black Country, near where I grew up in the English Midlands,' he told the Spaniard, 'it's seven years' bad luck if you meet *anyone* on the stairs.'

Borja chuckled. 'In Spain's case that would be forty years, I'm afraid. Four decades of tyranny.'

'He'll be dead soon, right? Franco? From what I've heard.'

The man looked to the heavens and held out his arms. 'This is the Month of the Most Precious Blood!'

He crossed himself.

'Am I wrong?'

'Wrong?' His eyes on Enoch. 'Sometimes we get what we pray for, don't we?'

'Do we?'

'Then we really *see*.'

'Oh ah.'

'That it's something else we wanted, after all.'

'That's just a reason to give up,' said Enoch.

'No,' replied the man, pulling a boarding pass from his linen jacket, 'it's a reason for going further.'

Enoch couldn't disagree on a day like today.

'That's what's so scary,' Borja continued.

Maybe there's more to a banister-clutcher than meets the eye.

As troop vehicles paraded in front of the main terminal, all assembled – Conquerors too – strained and leaned forward to discover who in fact was travelling inside that vehicle towards the rear of the party.

'Would it be Juan Carlos in the limo, then?' asked Enoch.

'Our king? No chance,' replied Borja. 'Franco's generals shrink his balls.'

'Only the chauffeur!' said a smartly dressed Catalan woman to her friend.

She was right.

The back seat was bare.

What theatre.

It was now plain as day, however, that the dusty combat vehicles and their regal-looking Mercedes were in fact escorting a set of Iberia boarding steps.

A staircase in the sweltering afternoon, heading out of the

airport compound, hauled by chains attached to a personnel carrier. Steps.

Enoch turned to look at his new travelling companion.

Borja was smirking.

'You saw them coming all along!' said Enoch.

'Of course.'

'You don't miss much.'

'I live in a country where vigilance pays.'

Enoch scratched his head. All Borja's chatter about famous stairs was prompted by what had been happening on the runway. Incredible. Enoch wasn't accustomed to being impressed by a man over thirty-five. 'There are easier ways to move airline steps,' he said.

'Not when Franco's involved.'

'But he's not here.'

'We live in the 1930s in Spain,' replied Borja.

'Come off it.'

'Nineteen seventy-four,' he said, 'and a flight of stairs brings Madrid's international airport to a standstill. Barajas is not quite Heathrow, is it?'

'Pity,' remarked Enoch. 'I wanted a peek at the famous dictator.'

'You got one,' he replied. 'Those stairs are for him. To practise walking for the cameras.'

Several British were ridiculing the military display, the sub-machine guns. More absurdity interfering with their Conquerors' 'Magic Summer Getaway (with free welcome cocktail).'

'Did I see him?' asked Enoch.

The man shook his head impatiently and indicated the security guards, who were saluting the boarding steps as they sailed out of the main gates to a waiting transporter. 'You did indeed. All but the flesh,' said Borja glumly. 'Quite enough for most.'

Enoch watched as the stairs were raised onto a flatbed vehicle.

'Do you have a place in Barcelona?' enquired the Spaniard.

'Yes,' said Enoch. Lying.

The man's fingers twirled at his beard. 'I was going to offer you a room above my Bar Andaluz in the Gothic quarter. My wife and daughter would be thrilled to have an Englishman stay for a few days.'

'Does it have stairs?'

'Hundreds,' he replied.

Even if Borja were up to something, this was the break Enoch needed. But the man frowned.

'All but the flesh,' he said reassuringly.

'What are steps for anyway?' replied Enoch.

And they waited in silence for the Iberia bus.

TRAVESTIS

Enoch realized he was two people: bruises attesting to one. But after a New Year celebration in Cadaqués, north of the city, he turned his back on *gay*, on shadows that lurked within, pursuing him on streets and into people's houses.

Five days a week, he worked diligently in Bar Andaluz off the Ramblas in the Gothic quarter. A wavering – but convincing enough – passion rose in him for Mireia whom he had met in Plaza Real nearby, shortly after arriving in Barcelona. The couple recognized their feelings as love. *Gay* was not his baby. In Mireia's eyes there had never been any doubt, as Enoch grew closer to the Gritte-d'Souza family, surrogate uncle to Mireia's younger brother and sister. Twins.

Normally, he would have spotted the item in *Vanguardia* or heard about it at Mireia's family home on Calle Balsareny or while serving tables. Forgotten the matter. You had to. More injustice, notched up to dictator Franco's ailing regime – and to the General's ever deteriorating health. El Caudillo's dying acts more desperate by the month. On Saturday, September 27, 1975 – the paper reported – a few miles from Barcelona in Cerdanyola, a firing squad had marched into line and aimed its pistols. Five men collapsed like rubble. Suspected terrorists found guilty after a series of implausible – some were saying audacious – military trials.

There should have been no connection, but late in the afternoon on the following Monday, unable to bear the sexual yearning, Enoch crossed the Ramblas to its seamier side: Calle Mina and the wrath, absolution of the Claustro Club – where all his denying found its home in pain.

At a rundown building – former Barrio Chino warehouse – was the men's hammam. On dimly lit upper floors, however, were tiled, high-ceilinged storage areas that the management termed Safe Houses. Enoch walked past the first, past open door-bolts and three men beyond – one naked lying in a leather hammock with latticework that allowed his ass to hang free; the other two in immaculate army uniforms standing beside a tub in the centre of the room.

When his courage was enough – standing in his paper-thin crimson towel – he walked back and entered. The men roused themselves as though a teammate had at last arrived. A painted skylight cast an eerie spic-and-span sheen over the middle of this space, made the enamel bathtub itself a performer. Illuminated stage.

One of the men came up behind Enoch, kissed his neck and forced him to his knees. Enoch opened his jaw in readiness. But the man moved aside – removing the youth's towel as he did so – tying a cord around Enoch's wrists. A military figure stepped up in front of him, lowered a studded dog-collar over Enoch's head. Secured it with the solemnity of a priest. Three men stood and considered their boy, his lowered eyes. Enoch's cock stiffening.

In a secret, hidden-away bathhouse, why did Enoch always think of Tintin? The sexless comic figure who never undressed. Every second ridding the world of villainy. Tintin the *ingénu*, determined, with Captain Haddock and dog Snowy at his beck and call. Tintin, private eye-newspaper reporter, always at odds – in action, observant – until the end of the story, mystery solved.

Pain is cautious too. Hunts. Watches. Creeps stealthily like a snake. Or detective. Criminal. Until everything but the pain is absurd and irrelevant. Tintin pain. Enoch, like Franco, greeting torment. Was compassion in all this? Gentleness? Snowy's part of the game? Wherever it was, in reaching these Safe House men, Enoch felt Tintin and Franco within his flesh – writhing. Like camouflage. Amidst bodies taut and rank with violation. And desire.

Followed by his two pals, the costumed army man strode out of the room, bolting its door shut. Enoch remained on his knees repeating a mantra: breathe, boy, breathe.... Several minutes later, the bolts flew open and in rushed three men, two naked, one in green military garb.

Bolts slammed shut.

No one spoke. Someone pulled a hood over Enoch's head, covering his eyes, face and neck in leather, laced tightly at the back; holes for the nostrils, zipper at the mouth.

Water runs into the bath....

Later that evening – in declining euphoria – Enoch walked past the Liceo opera house, Boquería market. He became aware that the crowds on Rambla Estudios were looking over their shoulders to Plaza Cataluña, threshold of the Ramblas.

Something was wrong.

The news kiosks shut down too early. Everything locked and shuttered, but in haste, it seemed: several awnings open, protecting nothing. No buskers, pavement artists or fortune tellers. On a regular evening?

People were not strolling. You didn't stroll like this.

It was the Sant Miquel festival in remembrance of Napoleon's occupation of Spain. Enoch knew that. But down in Barceloneta around the fish restaurants and port. A character called Bum Bum marched through the working-class neighbourhood to the sound of rifle shots.

On the Ramblas, traffic had drawn to a standstill. Motorists honked.

September was rife with annual Ramblas parades, many in defiance of El Caudillo's edicts. The indigenous language was banned. Nevertheless, on the eleventh was Diada, Catalan National Day; on the twenty-fourth, a week-long La Mercè with its *carrefoc* march of fire-spouting dragons, tree-high effigies and serpents, celebrating Our Lady of Mercy. A month of processions. Last of the dictator's tyranny over Spain, many hoped, but the previous year everyone had said the same: Franco's eulogy.

Behind Enoch, someone said, 'Oh, *travestís.*'

In the distance, a group of thirty or so transvestites emerged, swishing down the central promenade. One of the more unofficial parades normally confined to lower Rambla Santa Monica and the disreputable streets around Claustro Club, sailors' brothels, the Muscatel and *caçalla* bars.

'Faggots!' a kid shouted, climbing a lamppost.

Enoch's heart raced.

Ramblas spectators moved aside. Wolf whistles. Some applauding. A blown kiss. But the majority simply witnessed. Respectfully? Surely not. In surprise? Not a word on their lips. Maybe good-humoured contempt. Most men knew that boy-arse was safer and tighter – better still if it wore garters and silk panties. Spanish men weren't fussy. 'Siesta is siesta behind closed doors,' his friend Borja liked to say of the Ramblas sex trade. 'There's a reason for afternoon traffic on Rambla Santa Monica.'

You react *outside*, in the public eye, thought Enoch. Doors flung open. '*Travestís* are Spain's advance party,' Mireia had once explained. 'Everyone sees what happens to *them* first. Like rats in a lab.'

Just a minute. There were students too. Following. Those *travestís* were quite literally taking the lead. No scouting party at all.

It was the Cerdanyola executions. *A protest.*

Following on the ladies' stiletto heels was a phalanx of demonstrators as far as the eye could see, choking all entrances to Rambla Canaletes like the colossal dragons and effigies of the recent Mercè.

Thousands had taken to the streets.

Salvador Dalí – host of that New Year party in Cadaqués – had sent a telegram *congratulating* Franco for his decisiveness, Enoch recalled. He began hurrying towards the next side street. In the distance, placards jabbed at trees, Catalan flags and trades union banners hung in stifling air. Mobs singing. Chanting. Drums. As the cacophony rose, so people leaned from balconies. Transvestite rights were the least of it.

Whether anyone liked it or not, the *travestís* were in front of deep popular revulsion at Franco's killings.

The smile fell smartly from Enoch's face.

'Hostia,' he cursed.

This was no marching; these demonstrators were now running.

The Ramblas's head a swollen creek of people near *sprinting*. Frightened. Stumbling over tables and chairs. Spilling into narrow side streets. Vehicles abandoned on the pavement. Cars, buses, struggling to U-turn.

Gunfire crackled, echoing against brick and window. Protesters scattered like dust on water. Balconies cleared. Shutters thundered down. Catalan flags were tossed in the road, prison-bar posters of Franco. Party political pamphlets denouncing the recent executions. Screaming. Voices yelling directions. Bedlam.

A canister rolled against the side of a bookstall. Someone kicked it into a drain.

Run, Enoch! Cover your eyes.

More bullets slicing the air. Sharp *twang* above his head. Another and another. Ahead, a café's grille caved like tissue paper.

Out of breath, a woman in neckerchief and beret leaned against one of many plane trees, reaching for the small of her back. Friends tugged at her arm. She took three steps and fell on her face, blood seeping through her T-shirt. Enoch ran into the road.

An elderly man lay stone dead, clutching his neck.

No one stopped for anyone now.

Up there, Enoch! He ran for Calle Pintor Fortuny and an escape route to the Ronda, a main road. *Twang.* Shouting, more screams.

Military helmets, shields, and machine guns swarmed past the Plaza Cataluñya subway entrances.

As the tear gas cleared, your eyes made out riot police with batons, six in the middle of the square pounding a bald-headed man curled on the ground like a fiddlehead.

Water-cannon speeding into view from Calle Pelayo, firing at the huddled marchers until they slammed into litterbins and bushes like tumbleweed.

Officers rounded up leaders and bystanders alike, throwing them into unmarked vans.

Water rained like tickertape. Incongruous as *travestí* lamé.

Minutes later – ten, fifteen – Enoch, sodden, had run through the Barrio Chino red-light district to that Ronda, out to Gran Vía;

and from there into the fashionable shopping vicinity of Paseo de Gracia, safely into the principal Avenida Diagonal that diced the city in two.

Monday evening here, like any other. Restaurants serving dinner, solitary newspaper-readers, *boulevardiers*, women and men ambling, office workers still enjoying their time. Could you believe it? An elderly gentleman, not unlike the one lying dead on the Ramblas, feeding pigeons in a square. Bars open, cafés. Yellow and black taxis cruising for fares. Hadn't anyone heard the clamour? Did they think the shots Bum Bum?

Enoch felt shame. The *travestís* marching for their country. Spain. Not just Catalonia. Leading a parade. Warriors. While he played hard-on in a bathtub. Deceiving Mireia and her family. And himself.

The Claustro wasn't home.

It was guilt – not trust – with its pecker at someone's whip. The twinkle in a torturer's eye is not love. All he wants is to hurt, humiliate. You know that; but you don't *feel* it. You pretend he loves you.

Enoch's quaking had reached back, far beyond the night of meeting Mireia in Plaza Real. It was Guy Fawkes 1972: Enoch's Longbridge home in Birmingham, England; neighbours Nelly and Ted Barton with Austin worker friends in a party mood, flopping their wrists at him. Seventeen-year-old nancy-boy.

In his life he had turned away to an oasis as misleading as this Diagonal normality and calm, to a Claustro Club, and humiliation. His adoptive mother Vera had lived in the World Wars of her family. Spaniards had *their* Civil War. Enoch was beginning to see. Horror walked inside us – never took its leave.

As Mireia's father had once explained, Barcelona was at least three cities piled up like layers of lasagna. Tonight was supper toppled on its side, each stripe a country to itself. That's how it felt to Enoch: bands of pasta and hairstuck tomato. Awaiting a fork to scoop them up. Mouths open, closed.

But Mireia said it best at the New Year's party in that eccentric painter's Cadaqués home: you *engage* with darkness. Enoch had avowed it earlier in his upbringing, but had ducked the struggle. He needed to love a man. March proudly – in heels, if necessary. Lead. *Engage* with what so scared him.

He didn't need the Claustro any more.

Enoch had a face.

YOU DRESS UP, YOU DANCE

Jessica Manley's office was on the second floor of St. Catherine's House.

At noon, Enoch took the Circle Line from Sloane Square near his hotel – busy even in November with European and other visitors – to Temple on the Victoria embankment. It was overcast, mizzly. Enoch walked in haste along the Kingsway.

Puddles, taxis, pigeons.

Off London's Thames and around the stately edifices of Australia House and India House, a chill wind seeped through his flimsy alpaca jacket and made him shiver. Pedestrians' faces were averted against the cold, umbrellas tilted defiantly, clerical workers and Inns-of-Court barristers on lunch-hour dodged traffic to reach their pubs. Shoppers queued at bus stops. Enoch too restless to do anything but ensure St Catherine's House really stood where the letterhead indicated.

It did: 10, Kingsway. Mrs Manley's office assuredly inside. His appointment in five hours' time. Birth-mother news getting closer. Enoch stepped into the lobby to check office numbers. Nothing must go wrong at five o'clock. 'Search Rooms' off to one side were jammed with people. Notepads and pencils in their hands, researchers of every kind wandering library stacks. CRAMP territory – Council for the Reunion of Adoptees and their Missing Parents.

At scruffy tables, readers pored over gargantuan, Alice-in-Wonderland volumes. Small-print lists in oversize records, names and dates and serial numbers on the searchers' own paper scraps and on their lips. But no one – not even Dickens's Mr Pickwick or Uriah Heep – seemed to be discovering anything. The air was heavy with imaginings – turn of one page after another. A sense that other occupations might be worth the time.

Enoch returned to the street. Wandered. Hunched against the rain.

Over a year ago – before his moonlight flit to Barcelona – he had lived a few months above Riaz Mansour's Cable Street fish-and-chip shop in Whitechapel. Enoch had never ventured far from work, other than to Spitalfields Market, Petticoat Lane at weekends, the Blind Beggar for a Saturday night pint with Riaz. His boss called it the 'poofter palace' because one of the Kray twins, Ronnie, had killed a mobster on its premises for calling him a fruit. Riaz hated fags.

Not often, Enoch would hit the West End or walk by the Tower of London and the river. Mostly he stayed local, even read the novels Chubbsy mailed from Enoch's former halfway house in Brighton: E. M. Forster's *Passage to India*, Thomas Hardy's *Jude the Obscure*, Charles Dickens's *Bleak House*. More grim Sassoon. It was a life. Enoch thought it bearable – but not his lot. Then the Spain courier-errand came up. How he hoped Riaz would not eat out today, or that Major Chubb were in town. They must have felt deeply betrayed by his absconding – and with all their dreams and architectural drawings, bestowed on some dumper in Barcelona's Gothic quarter.

Nostalgia, self-recrimination would not do this afternoon, however. Time for new turf. Enoch looked around the corner. This corner, at his feet. Where was he? He was in Holborn. He would explore Holborn. No sooner had he crossed into Lincoln's Inn Fields – a world of law as remote as his detention centre on the Blanchland moors – voices returned, indignant at his treatment of men, women, children, who had cared about him. Voices barely held at bay for the hours they rattled him. Where was he going? Neglecting them so?

The streets became gloomier, buildings inhospitable. Enoch turned from the Inns of Court where Margaret Thatcher had studied to steps beside the London School of Economics. In front of him was a board listing LSE's famous alumni. One of the Rolling Stones was amongst them! Enoch gaped at the name. How could Jagger do that? Go to a university all about money? Do I know *anything* about

England? How come I didn't know about Inns of Court and LSE? Obviously, everyone else does.

Voice. Voices.

As five o'clock drew near, the talking in his head became louder and more combative. More recrimination. Collywobbles. Enoch hoped that Barcelona, Mireia, the Mediterranean had not softened him. Not since Blanchland House and Chubbsy's Sassoon Lodge had he dealt with Social Services. Tear gas, but not *counsellors*. All he wanted to do was pass the 'I'm not going to butcher my birth-ma' screening. That was what the *interview* was about. Someone's theoretical model needed airing. It was worse than politics.

Enoch leaned hard against the wall outside Room 208, St. Catherine's House, as though walking backwards against traffic in Piccadilly Circus. Please, stop speaking to me. *Please.*

'Enoch Jones?'

STOP.

Five o'clock in the afternoon.

STOP.

Enoch quietened in an instant at Jessica Manley's welcome. Her mellifluous voice did it, and the way she so nonchalantly held an astonishing FUCK YOU I'M BLACK mug of coffee, warming her hands prayerfully under the institutional lights.

Requisitely marginalized as an English-Jamaican of colour, Jessica Manley exchanged looks with expatriate trailer-trash. How cosy and philanthropic she seemed. Her beige shawl and woollen skirt made him think of country walks and spaniels; her beads, *ganja*, peace and winter cruises. She seemed kindly. Composed. Surely not the effects of an adolescence spent on LSD? Wise, all-seeing. Middle age triumphantly bluffing death.

Give it up, Enoch.

He felt utterly at her mercy. She had in her possession everything he wanted. Jessica was an icon. He couldn't screw up, couldn't let her detect his temperament. Would he get his pilot's licence? She observed him while appearing not to. Enoch had met the technique before, caught many an interrogator peering at all the wrong-right moments – when you needed to choke something back or conjure up an acceptable story about some personal trauma. They microscopicked you – pieced x with y whenever you blinked – and waited for Atlantis to rise from the seabed.

'No-nonsense mug,' quipped Enoch, trying to soothe his nerves.

'Thank you,' she replied, in a comradely way. People must notice the logo every time – cute 101 tool for bringing anxious clients down to earth. 'From Woodstock.'

'*The* Woodstock?' he replied. 'You're American?'

'My mother is. Father's British.'

Lordy, lordy. 'A response to the white man who bashed your people first?'

'Good, isn't it?' She smiled, therapeutically. Patient was relaxin'. Mug worked. 'The irony is I take milk in my freshly ground.'

Humour. Engagement. The fireworks could begin.

For a moment, he wondered what Catalan social workers drank out of. FUCK YOU I GAROTTE NOT? Was there any way of comparing? He felt like one of *Dr Who*'s robotic Daleks from childhood television. Was Barcelona worse than Longbridge? I COULD LINE INNOCENT PEOPLE UP AGAINST A WALL AND SHOOT THEM mug? SPEAK MY OWN LANGUAGE? MAKE PEOPLE DISAPPEAR? You'd need more than one mug for Spain.

'Enoch,' she said abruptly. Not quite clicking her fingers. 'Down to brass tacks: you want to find your birth mother.'

Even the way she said his name. With a lilting Caribbean accent that spoke of knowledge he did not own; journeys taken and to come. Enoch felt his knees trembling.

'First let me congratulate you for arriving at this decision to find your beginnings – and the name of your birth mother. It's your right. But it must have been difficult making up your mind to search?'

She paused for the tease and tweak. As client, you're supposed to pour forth in these gaps. But its always more telling if you let the *counsellor* pour first. Anything to derail the script, find stronger limbs to cling to.

'Enoch?'

Jessica was on a production line, though. Enoch reasonably secure. 'Appointments knee-high,' he had heard her say to a colleague, after inviting him in. He'd get what he wanted. She wasn't at home. Not really.

'No,' was the best answer. Enoch confided that he wished only to meet his mother. That was all. His adoptive mother – Vera Jones – was not comfortable about the tracing but had *agreed*. Enoch dressed himself in un-avenging weeds with un-axeman-like gestures. His birth parent would be safe with him.

In her Home Counties hippy turn, Jessica reminded Enoch that in 1955 his mother would have been told that adopted children would never be shown their original names. Such was the legislation.

'I understand.'

Jessica bending forward. This means *serious* bit. Maybe his eyes had been shooting all over her office, just like those of Mike Malin, his phys. ed. instructor at Blanchland House. She was targeting the hoop. 'There are many reasons why your mother may not wish to meet you, Enoch. No one in her family may be aware of your existence, for example – she would have to tell them, and her husband if he does not know. If he *does* know, it will have been a taboo subject. That's our usual finding.'

Jessica sipped her coffee, eyes up like a frog. But he was ready, nodding so very sanely. How well balanced and mature. Sound in mind and body. On the coach trip from Barcelona, he had prepared *intelligent, even-handed,* though he felt neither. He was hiding *ruthless*, though certain he did not feel that either – yet. *Desperation* he'd successfully hidden from himself until this moment. *Anger* at his mothers, fathers – anger that would have the decency to remain submerged for a while longer. At least until he had left Jessica's office. Enoch allowed his eyes to blink slowly.

Frog to frog.

'Sometimes birth mothers think compensation is a factor in reunions. For them or for the child. But Enoch, in your letter you tell me this isn't so?'

'Right. Just meet and that's it. Let her see I'm okay. I get to look at someone I resemble.'

'Yes,' said Jessica, hesitating with due concern. There were lines still to deliver: 'Your mother may be jittery about who needs to know of the adoption – and who may find out. Also, you will likely remind your mother of your father, her lover. This man is *not* her current husband. Feelings will run high.'

'Her husband might belt me one, you mean?'

'Or her. Or both of you. Have you thought how you might react if your birth mother declines to see you, Enoch?'

Enoch stared at Jessica. It was *the* question. Truth was he'd track her down, stalk her, and at least get a gander. Maybe ask her for a light. Get near. See her face and clothes. Just to smell. Probably that would be enough. But you don't tell a social worker that. Ensuing therapy would take months. Jessica Manley might not put out.

'Be disappointed. But continue my life,' he said. 'Consoling myself that I'd made the attempt to find her.'

Jessica nodded again. Shyster, was she thinking?

'Maybe this is not a good idea, after all,' said Enoch. 'Is that your point?'

'Not at all, Enoch,' she replied. 'Of course you want to find your natural parent. These are simply matters to bear in mind when you do so. Not every mother wishes to be reminded of the son she gave away, does she? Let's examine what information we do have, though; that will fill you in on who you are.'

Let's.

From her overloaded desk, she picked up an envelope and slid out a thin wad of documents.

'I have to go and photocopy some other materials for you, Enoch. But while I'm gone, why not read these first?'

She sifted through the pages, careful not to hand them over quite yet.

'There are the Children's Visitor Reports from May 16th 1955 to July 15th, when you first went to Vera and Frank Jones's home in Bloxwich in the Black Country. The visitor Frances Cunningham reviews your new environment and, together with a Birmingham guardian *ad litem* who also makes visits, she supervises your adoption until the Juvenile Court approves it. In your case, this happened in August 1955. The adoption was arranged by Lichfield Diocesan Association for Moral Welfare. That's at Rickerscote House in Staffordshire. The court hearing for some reason was in Henley-in-Arden, on the other side of Birmingham. Backlogs, I suppose. Your case went where there was availability.'

Jessica left the handwritten papers on a table next to him – and quietly closed the door. Enoch looked upon the sheets, reaching down into the ink:

Mr and Mrs Frank Jones live in a full size caravan on this Bloxwich site, properly planned in a field behind Natsfield Farm, midway between the Wyrley-Essington canal and Bealeys Lane. Enoch has been very good on the whole and is on Ostermilk II. He was in the pram outside the caravan. Nicely dressed. Blankets clean and tidy. Vera Jones is a pleasant, homely woman. She has never had a child of her own and is very delighted that they have been able to adopt....

Enoch was unaware of just how long Jessica's photocopying had taken. But as he completed a third reading, she entered the room. He could not look up, but now guessed there had been no copying.

He hid his face.

Enoch is now 15 lbs. In the shade of a big tree fast asleep. He obviously receives good care and affection.

Tears were spilling down Enoch's cheeks.

Enoch now weighs over 17 lbs, is firm and looks contented and healthy. Mrs Jones obviously takes great pride in him. They have postponed their summer holiday until September 3rd, after the court date. Mrs Jones has lavished love and attention on Enoch but has not spoilt or coddled him. She seems so delighted to have a baby to care for.

Without missing a beat, Jessica came to Enoch's side and placed her hand upon his back. His body shook. The game up. Together, they looked in silence at the four pages of Visitor Reports. His eyes stinging. Frances Cunningham's neatly levelled penmanship. The ink ebony black, as though written yesterday.

Enoch now weighs over 18 lbs and is a big, rather fat baby. He sleeps well, has started cereals which he enjoys. Strong and active. Mrs Jones was out for the morning and her mother was in charge of the baby. The guardian ad litem has visited. An adoption hearing has been set for August 31st at Henley Juvenile Court. Garden plot is well tended.

How careful Jessica was. How helpless he felt.

'Big news, isn't it?' she said, returning to her desk and sitting down. 'I know it's difficult, Enoch. Really I do. But wonderful news.'

'Thanks,' he replied, wiping his flushed face.

'The rest, I'm afraid, is disappointing.'

Enoch nodded. Still feeling as though he had let himself down, sobbing in front of a social worker.

'You know that I cannot give you your original birth certificate but here are the forms. With them you'll be able to pick it up downstairs on your way out. We've extended Search Room hours pending the new Acts of Parliament.'

Again, she delayed the handing over. 'As you saw on the Visitor Reports, your original name was Enoch Joseph *Smith*.'

'Vera Jones my adoptive mother didn't give me those first names?'

Jessica paused. 'The name recorded on your original birth certificate – which no one, including yourself, has ever seen, is "Enoch Joseph Smith." Nancy Smith, your birth mother chose both your names.' She paused again. 'Vera Jones told you otherwise?'

Enoch could not speak. In this, Vera had also misled him.

'It's not uncommon for an adoptive mother to protect the birth mother, Enoch. Vera could well have been simply trying to uphold the spirit of the law, that an adopted child would never have access to identifying facts. Why trouble you? That may have been her reasoning.'

Enoch bowed his head again, let the moment pass.

'Your natural mother was Nancy Hannah Smith. Her address is given as 37, Paddock Lane, Walsall. Your father is not mentioned. This too is very usual. You were born at New Cross Hospital, Wolverhampton, on March 31st, 1955.'

'Wolverhampton?'

'Nancy Smith was probably a very young teenager, Enoch. In those days, her Walsall family – a foster one, I believe – would not have wanted the pregnancy or childbirth known to their local community.'

'Stigma.'

'Families didn't move house much, at that time – 1955. Nancy's reputation would have lasted a lifetime. My guess is that for the latter part of her confinement and for the actual delivery, she was taken to a different part of the Black Country for reasons of propriety. Wolverhampton was a common choice for girls in your mother's situation – or Birmingham – provided of course their families did not reside there.'

The back had fallen off Enoch's history. He could see himself prior to Vera Jones and Frank Jones. Prior to Graham Dagg, Vera's second man. At last. The missing pieces. *Before Christ*, and *After Death*.

Jessica passed the typed sheet to Enoch. There was a Wolverhampton address for Nancy Smith's mother: 'H. Smith. North Road.'

His heart skipped.

'Look here!' said Enoch. 'Forty-eight, North Road.'

'I know. That's what's so disappointing, Enoch,' she said. 'I checked with Wolverhampton, Walsall and Birmingham Central library archives. 'North Road was demolished years ago. It's a bypass now. Chances are it wasn't Nancy Smith's mother's home anyway: 48, North Road was more likely part of the Adoption Society as 37, Paddock Lane probably was. Mother and Baby hospices were numerous. There is little chance that either Nancy or her mother would have had their actual places of residence recorded on any official document.'

Enoch's voices chattered excitedly. He must have looked downcast by the commotion.

'I know I sound discouraging, Enoch. But I've been in this occupation for a long time, and there are distinct patterns to the treatment of pregnant girls in the 1950s. Nevertheless, there *are* 1954–5 Electoral Registers for Paddock Lane and for North Road. You could start looking in those of course. New Cross Hospital in Wolverhampton may still have admissions records.'

'I've got her name, and mine,' said Enoch – as though Jessica might take them away again. 'That's fantastic. Thank you.'

'Our office checked with Staffordshire and Wolverhampton Social Services, which house the records of the now defunct Lichfield Diocesan Association for Moral Welfare. Nothing came up. I wasn't surprised, the adoption agencies had to keep records for only fifteen years. Henley-in-Arden Juvenile Court no longer exists, and there weren't any records at Birmingham, Solihull or Stratford courts.'

'So I give up?'

'Oh no. This is all quite usual. CRAMP can help you. You've heard of that organization, you told me in your letter. They offer support, research assistance, intermediaries and so on. Also, here is a list of Post-Adoption Societies in England and Wales, should you think you've located Nancy Smith. Who, by the way, will have a different surname if she has married.'

Jessica glanced at the twilit drizzle of the courtyard. A sadness came over her as though she were becalmed, for a moment, by these hide-and-seek mothers, as indistinct as the slate-grey London beyond her window. 'You'll need an intermediary, should you think you've found Nancy – and the Post-Adoption Society in her area will help you, and try to arrange a meeting.'

'What if she's in Scotland?'

'Use the Yellow Pages, Enoch,' she said abruptly, her hand dismissive. 'The Scots are a law unto themselves. I never understand....'

General Franco neither. Separatists.

'You now have names to go on. It won't be easy finding your birth mother but it's certainly more feasible now. Nevertheless, I should tell you that there is a likelihood that no further information exists about Nancy or yourself. You are twenty years old, Enoch – an adult. Think seriously about ever tracking her down, won't you? That these names might be sufficient knowledge?'

'Okay.'

Jessica was right. Nancy was another person in the world. No matter what. Wouldn't that be enough?

Hello, Nancy Smith. I'm Enoch. Remember me?

Jessica smiled and shook Enoch's hand. Tonight was clearly overtime – her next client already seated outside the door. A shy and harried Asian woman with an expensive-looking raincoat. Struggling to remove an LHR airline baggage tag from her briefcase, she studied Enoch as you might the menu on a first date.

'Don't forget to collect the certificate,' Jessica said, pointing to a floor directory near the lift. 'It's what you came for, remember?'

Social workers were the lost tribe. But worked on you like soapy baths and Ovaltine. Enoch pressed 'Ground,' watching as Jessica disappeared into her office followed by the rainspotted woman who, for some reason, tossed the LHR tag onto the floor. Maybe he would change his view of the social work profession – its theories and practice – after today. About time. You just wondered what they were like with *people*. Outside in a downpour. Or on a London tube.

Maybe it didn't matter.

You dress up, you dance.

ONCE UPON A PRISSY

On Thursday night around eleven, Enoch decided to leave Bar Andaluz for a few hours and get started. Since his return from London – and the discovery of his birth mother's name – he persuaded himself that more trips to England would be necessary. Even likely. It was early December, 1975. He needed much more money to repay Mireia and Borja for the last visit, and a stash to help him respond to news he hoped was imminent.

When Enoch crossed the Ramblas at Escudellers, he hadn't planned to do much more than track down a few *pensiones* that Borja had recommended, and get a sense of the neighbourhood he would adopt for his new enterprise. One that Mireia would have abhorred, and Borja – though amused – tried to de-glamorize. Unsuccessfully.

Enoch wandered for an hour along the Paralelo, amidst hordes of neon-lit bars and dance halls already in full swing – and entered the heart of Barrio Chino, turning left up San Olegrio where a line of women seated on folding chairs or standing, some knitting or crocheting, one peeling vegetables, awaited their customers and listened to the radio.

One of the seated – in her fifties and stolid – lifted her widow's skirt for Enoch. He took a long look at the shaved, clipped cunt he was offered and hurried on. A younger mulatta, dressed in pink silk, leapt forward with prices in her grin as she fumbled at Enoch's crotch. '*Maricón*,' he said. First time the word to describe himself, in any language, had left his lips. Faggot. The woman chuckled, repeating it to her friend who was idly adjusting a black choker.

Along from San Olegrio the streets became even narrower, the passersby more down-at-heel and swarthier, fretworked with Andalusian sun – and hopelessness. The cramped slum buildings were more forbidding than on the wider working-class streets, the ever-present stench of piss, rotting fruit, coffee and sewers more powerful. Enoch walked by rooming-houses with children spilling out. Laundry at the windows. Men with nothing to do. His idea would never work here. Too many eyes; too much danger.

Pensión Sol was at the corner of San Jeronimo and San Bartolomé – well off the tourist-beaten track – and clearly a dive of the first order with low entrance and peeling shutters. Flies, dogs. Yet few people about – and those who shifted by were more concerned with their own business to worry about a limey twenty-year-old scouting out a lair. It'll do, he thought. No one's going to find me down here. Enoch would try his luck at peseta-making just like the ladies down the road. He found the prospect exhilarating. Tomorrow he'd return and book a room with monthly rates.

But where do rent-boys rent?

He knew from Borja that transvestites and more theatrical, old-men-in-powder-and-rouge homosexuals paraded along Arco del Teatro and at the lower end of the Ramblas. So that was where he headed, stopping for a bottle of San Miguel and a plate of *frites* in a squalid Muscatel bar – Molino – across from the Drassanes shipyards. He watched Calle Madrona for a while, bought a packet of Ducados from a kid who was working tables, and headed onto Rambla Santa Monica – now, after midnight, bustling and raunchy.

No use trying to get into one of the groups of *travestís* hanging about American marines who littered both sides of the Ramblas, so he stood with a small crowd gathered about a pavement artist chalking up Madonna and Child in pastels – and earning very little. Enoch watched the watchers of the *travestís* – men, lingering. Trade in process between the Rambla Santa Monica and the direction of Calle Madrona. Enoch followed a transvestite and her john, witnessing how the pleasure-circus ran. How could anyone miss it? Several adjacent houses on Madrona – four of them – were brothels for all to see.

Enoch caught the eye of a middle-aged man, wavy hair brushed back from his forehead, paunchy, dressed in cotton trousers and obviously … looking. Enoch sidled up.

The festive-looking gent uttered something amiable in a Spanish accent Enoch could not follow.

'*Inglés*,' muttered Enoch.

The john looked this young Brit up and down and said something else. Enoch had underestimated the crucial role of vocabulary to this occupation. But a few phrases – or impenetrable slang – would not defeat him. He knew some Spanish and Catalan from his Bar Andaluz waitering and from Mireia and her family uptown, where he was now living intermittently. Sleeping other nights above Borja's bar. Surely he could get by in any language – and on any bed.

Enoch indicated they should move away. Not exactly sure where. Pensión Sol was too distant for a heavyset man. Somewhere nearer would have to do.

The elegant fellow hesitated. Rubbed his fingers.

'*Dos mil*,' said Enoch feeling very savvy. He had mastered most Spanish numbers. Key ones. Two thousand pesetas was around twenty pounds, certainly a going rate in London, he thought.

Playfully, the man rocked his head side to side. Then laughed – a flicker of gold tooth.

In the balmy evening, they walked along Calle Madrona to the nearest and seediest-looking pensión – Colón – and strolled in, prey at Enoch's side.

'*Cama*,' said Enoch, with panache. '*Una noche*.'

The owner looked uncertain as Enoch signed for one night's bed at seven hundred pesetas. But Enoch lacked the guts – or really, the terminology – to negotiate an hourly rate at frequent intervals. This money was the last of his Spanish banknotes. The john said nothing as Enoch handed over his passport. Man and boy shuffled up gloomy stairs to the third floor, and entered a room, which would have embarrassed even a detention centre: single bedstead, dresser, bare tawny-coloured light bulbs. Patina of dust over everything. The street below was choked with traffic and crowds heading to and from the Ramblas. The floor smelt of bleach. And sex.

The bellied, dandyish guy closed the door and adjusted his short-sleeved shirt. In the amber light, Enoch began to strip – get this man going, trying to ignore that the john was holding out his hand.

The rusty-coloured fellow said something more in his incomprehensible Spanish. Were his words even Spanish? Enoch tried to look quizzical as well as seductive, but the john rubbed his fingers again. '*Pesetas*,' he said, enunciating so very clearly for the English dumbshell.

Was this a menopausal rent-boy mugger?

'No,' said Enoch, scoffing as he raised his own hand. 'You give *me*.' He pointed to his hairless, acne-mapped torso.

The stranger let out a snort. '*Dos mille*,' said the john, beckoning.

'No,' replied Enoch. He lowered his jeans and tired underwear to create the fullest impact.

'*Mil quinientas*,' announced the john, puffing his own chest a little. One thousand five hundred.

The price was falling. 'Give. Give,' said the man impatiently, stabbing at the palm of his hand. 'Give mow-ney. Here. Give.'

Enoch stared in disbelief – and pointed into his own hand. 'NO. YOU. GIVE. ME.'

The two adversaries glared at one other.

Enoch's dick began to droop.

Suddenly the man spat, cursing the boy furiously, and dashed out of the room, slamming the door.

Enoch stood open-mouthed, his threadbare Wranglers and briefs around his ankles. The john thought Enoch was a virgin in need of deflowering? Was that it?

Little more to learn yet, Nell Gwynne, he thought after a few minutes, suspecting there'd be no refund on the room.

But Enoch wasn't eliminated so easily. In fact, he resolved to turn the situation right around. He couldn't be that incompetent; he was educated.

So this time when Enoch headed towards Rambla Santa Monica – waving touristically at the uneasy desk clerk as he left the seven hundred-pesetas-a-night-room – he took a good look at everyone but the *travestís*. He made eye contact with men, ambled about more effeminately than was his nature, and simpered his way through the early hours.

Got absolutely nowhere.

Sometime around 4 a.m., he decided to return to Pensión Colón. At a loss, Enoch couldn't fathom what was wrong – apart from not dressing as a woman.

On Calle Madrona he stopped again at the Molino bar and, with the last of his loose change, ordered beer. There was a small group of people inside: a drunk U.S. marine fresh from some blowout or other; a couple of hookers; and by the window, an Arab in his thirties, interested in nothing and no one.

A barman who'd seen better days – his attention mostly on the street, a half-gone cheroot between his lips – was talking to himself. Enoch took out yet another Ducados – and worked on his prospects.

Maybe he would leave Barcelona for good, if Borja and Mireia would loan him more bus fare back to England. He was losing his touch at Mireia's family home on Calle Balsareny – soon they would understand he was no match for their treasured daughter. There was always the dole in Britain. Even Major Chubbsy's halfway house might take him back, if he concocted some story. As a last resort, there was Vera and Graham in Birmingham, his adoptive mother and stepfather. He was not without options for a brilliant adulthood – and a birth mother quest he had kept so hidden from everyone, until lately.

Enoch pondered for nearly an hour before realizing that the Arab at the door was observing him. Enoch acknowledged the glance and, to his surprise, the misery walked over. Enoch invited him to smoke at the table. They sat – understanding there was little point attempting conversation beyond the fact that the man was from Algeria, and Enoch, England. But this did seem of interest to the older one who, after butting out his cigarette, tapped Enoch's arm and indicated they should leave.

On the street, his new acquaintance introduced himself.

'Ahmed,' he said, gripping his own shoulder. Enoch responded – and together they crossed the Ramblas to its Bar Andaluz side, and Barcelona's Gothic quarter. Just a block from the main railway station, past military guards outside an imposing building – they reached a typical cheek-by-jowl street lined with budget hotels.

As Ahmed and Enoch were about to enter Hotel America, a student dosshouse with backpackers' towels and sleeping-bags hanging over its balconies, Enoch stopped his guide and demonstrated – by pulling out empty pockets – that he was penniless. The Arab nodded – as though he already knew – and strutted in to the young woman at the front desk who barely raised her head from *Mundo* magazine. He uttered a few words – one of them *'quince'* – and, with key, the two new guests entered a ground-floor room the size of a single bed. A three-inch strip of mirrored tile surrounded the room at pillow level as though floor and ceiling were bejewelled into place.

Ahmed then giggled, and began to mime the massaging of Enoch's genitals and his own. Enoch was puzzled – and dropped down heavily on the bed. Everyone in this city was bizarre. Ahmed continued his pretence of undoing Enoch's pants and going down upon his – quite unexposed – penis. The Arab then tittered some more – and made a show of removing his own clothes. Without removing.

Enoch had endured enough, tonight – and abruptly reached for the door.

'Pesetas,' whispered Ahmed, grabbing his wrist, as though the word meant 'listen.' Like a conjuror, he made a circular movement with his hand and held up three fingers. Ahmed wanted three thousand pesetas. Thirty quid.

For that?

Enoch giggled himself.

'Mañana. Bar Molino,' said Ahmed. He displayed ten fingers pointing to Enoch's watch. *'Noche.'* Night. Ten p.m.

What a cretin. He thinks I'll turn up. Thirty quid for abracadabra? 'Fine, Ahmed.'

They headed out, past the magazine-reading woman. But not

before the Arab made Enoch observe his handing her a rolled three hundred pesetas – and key – for the use of room 15.

At the Ramblas, he held Enoch's arm tightly. With the other hand, he pressed a finger into the boy's throat. 'Bar Andaluz. Calle Vidrio. Borja Muñoz.' Ahmed was serious about payment. But when the Algerian also said, 'Mireia Gritte-d'Souza, Calle Balsareny,' Enoch swallowed hard. How did this stranger know his two addresses? How could someone so impotent and ridiculous be this sharp?

Grasping Enoch's arm even more cruelly, he twisted him like a dancer and sent him puppy-like on his way up the Ramblas. '*Buenas noches, inglesa,*' he said sibilantly, another titter in the night.

When Enoch arrived, scared and toil-worn, at his seven-hundred-peseta room at Pensión Colón – in debt for three thousand more – he sat looking at the ceiling bulb.

Suddenly – birdbrain that he was – Enoch realized he'd just attended rent-boy school.

On credit, Ahmed had shown him the ropes.

It was 6 a.m. Despairing, relieved – he wasn't sure – Enoch fell upon the mattress. You know what to do now – more or less – his voices told him. No words needed: English, Spanish or anything else. Just a few gestures and a price. Action. Enoch now knew where to take a john. It's going to be okay, those voices repeated. Ahmed's okay.

Later that morning, Enoch left Pensión Colón and headed again for the Ramblas, passport safely tucked into his jeans. In the lukewarm rain that had been falling since first light, he felt cleansed somehow – and determined once more to make his way in this godforsaken city. Last night, along Calle Madrona, Ahmed had indicated a small shop – with grilles on the tinted windows and coloured plastic strips in the doorway – that seemed to do a roaring trade in brown paper bags, judging by the men entering and leaving. Ahmed had said nothing at the time – merely nudged Enoch as they passed.

He'd start there.

The huddled premises were no disappointment: full with only

ten or so men, in their forties and fifties, respectable-looking and well fed, very unlike the characters you met elsewhere in the Barrio Chino. It was indeed a magazine store – shelves lined with well-fingered pornography. Stairs at the far end led to another room which, he discovered, was for queer clientele – another twelve or so, this morning making their selections.

Of one and all.

Enoch began browsing, placing himself next to a man whose eyes had not left Enoch's arse since he joined this happy library upstairs. Enoch's hands were unsteady – as much from hunger as nerves – while he flipped through a German nudist booklet: gangs of muscular, rock-hard cover boys.

Enoch closed a magazine. Leaned across to put the German hard-ons in their rack, deliberately brushing his neighbour's forearm. He glanced at the man's face. The slender, perspiring features nodded indiscreetly. Easy, this line of work. Silent, Enoch headed downstairs – past a vigilant and *bespectacled* Ahmed who was manning the cash machine.

So this *was* central station.

In a humid midday, Enoch walked ahead of the stripling of a john in Italian sandals, leading him directly to Hotel America. Enoch strolled into the lobby and its chipped tile floor. A huddle of North American backpackers – designer-casual in running shoes, T-shirts – was exuberantly and with great humour pocketing its Michelin maps and rail passes, heading out to the sliver of pavement. Yesterday's *Mundo*-reading girl had been replaced by a sober-looking gentleman in his sixties wearing a tie and shirt, greasy at the collar. Enoch gave a sidelong glance to rooms on the ground floor.

'*Quince*,' he said quietly, but with emphasis.

The man made a quick study of this shabby, foreign-looking twenty-year-old and scowled. Enoch indicated the rooms a second time. It wasn't going to work; the man was hesitating. Enoch prepared to scarper, eyeing the exit. Laboriously, the elderly receptionist lifted a key from its numbered cubbyhole. Enoch snatched it up and led the way – as a frequenter might do.

The rest was a cakewalk.

Afterwards, Enoch presented the front desk with a rolled-up three hundred pesetas – just as Ahmed had done – the remaining two thousand seven hundred nestling safely against his crotch. Not a word had passed between the john and Enoch, not even the price – three fingers in the air and a stiffy was all it took.

Four times that day – stopping only because he was sore and fantasies dried up – Enoch repeated his traffic between the Calle Madrona magazine store and Hotel America. By early evening, he had earned ten thousand, eight hundred pesetas – over a hundred pounds! Hotel America was richer by twelve hundred.

How simple, immorality. A lucky devil did look down on Barcelona, after all.

At ten o'clock that evening, after a sumptuous paella on Barceloneta waterfront, his underclothes rancid and crammed with folded banknotes, Enoch made the rendezvous at Bar Molino with Ahmed who was already waiting.

The Algerian ordered something – it sounded like 'ajenjo'. The barman placed two shot glasses below the counter and drizzled dark yellow liquor over a sugar cube held in miniature tongs. The process took a long time. When he'd finished, the barman returned this unmarked bottle to its cupboard – and presented the two men with their drinks.

Ahmed raised his glass and swigged. Enoch followed the man's lead.

'Jiggy jiggy good?' said Ahmed. 'Fairy boy?'

Enoch nodded – the drink was like nothing he'd ever tasted. Heavy, like a brandy that had gone off.

'Jiggy jiggy, fucky fucky,' repeated Ahmed, raising his eyebrows expectantly. 'You understan'?' He held out his palm. Ahmed really did want his three thousand peseta tuition. Enoch reached into his jeans and paid.

Ahmed smiled – and looked around the bar, before pocketing the money. 'Jiggy jiggy,' he began slowly, as though telling a story, 'twelve hundred pesetas me, three hundred pesetas Hotel America, fifteen hundred pesetas you. Understan'?'

Enoch finished his drink – now realizing it was absinthe – and stood up, knocking over a chair.

Ahmed jumped to his feet and leaned in close.

'Fuck off,' said Enoch.

Ahmed showed him a blade.

Enoch kneed him and made to run.

'*Puta i Raimoneta*,' hissed Ahmed in Catalan, pursing his lips mockingly. *Prissy whore.*

He grabbed Enoch's neck, slamming the boy's head against their table.

'Okay,' said Enoch, choking. He was no John Wayne.

There was no use battling. The Algerian was armed as well as stoned.

Ahmed pulled him up close. 'Shop. Magazine. One, two, three, four times.' He counted it out in a glutinous accent, baring his teeth with every number. 'Twelve hundred, plus twelve hundred, plus twelve hundred, plus twelve hundred. Hm?'

The Arab wanted four thousand eight hundred pesetas. He caught Enoch's glance towards the door – and slammed his pasty English face into a shelf.

'Okay, okay,' gasped Enoch, blood oozing from his nose.

Again, he reached inside his underwear and paid.

What with seafood dinner and the booze he'd put down between johnfucks, Enoch was left with one thousand five hundred pesetas. Fifteen quid for a day's whoring.

'Good night, fairy-tale,' scoffed Ahmed. 'I got your number, man.'

Enoch headed for Bar Andaluz and some sleep, consoling himself that he still had *some* money. Tomorrow he would return to Calle Madrona. Tomorrow and tomorrow. England – mother-search – on the radar once again.

It might all be fairy story.

But he was in.

PART THREE

SUMMAT ELSE

Walsall, England. 1954

A murmur it was.

In the grate.

Hopthrust fairy or a god or that solitary next-door Widow Caddlestone, griping and whispering. But there again. Was it cursing, pleading or comforting? Through the leafy, cheap, pee-yellow wallpaper and the handspan laminated mantel above the fireplace.

Calling in that hushed, from-another-room way.

Out of the grate or out of the girl's own skull? Fifteen-year-old Nancy Smith, in her faded pink-roses nightdress, couldn't make head or tail of it. Not a syllable.

So she knelt down at the empty hearth – beneath the glass Siamese cats, deer, bunny-clusters, and a miniature copper Blackpool ashtray or two, and leaned inside – like a Lob-Lie-by-the-Fire, the awkward breed of ugly goblin her *real* mother once told her about, who caused soot to fall in stews, made bread heavy, and upset the gaga girls' needlework. There it was again – a voice – muttering and questioning as though in conversation with itself now.

Uncle Albert Mallinder is coming at 5 a.m. – to mind you for two weeks, Nancy. Mabel and Edwin Proffit your foster parents say so. But you don't believe them, do you? You know who's really coming. You know who'll be knocking at the door of number 10 Kendrick Road. At five o'clock in the morning.

What a trouble these interruptions.

But truth to tell, Nancy's thoughts were more on the particular *day* it was than on the shenanigans, wherever they came from, echoing in her ears.

Saturday, July 24th, 1954 – 'Genesis, dear,' as Nancy's foster mother called it. 'Day the world begins for the likes of us,' she would say. She would have to say, over and over, before actually leaving Walsall. 'Two blessed weeks when everything gets sorted out.'

Or else.

So on a day like today you could expect *anything*: cinders flying out of a grate, women in curlers and Nivea cold cream stirring mugs of tea, but with jigged bonehandle knives. Even from Widow Caddlestone next door – Kendrick Road's two-up-two-down washday-week gossip – raking coals at first light on a summer's day was not out of the question. So maybe the noise *was* her alone; in fact, wouldn't you expect Mrs Caddlestone to be up to something?

So Nancy hesitated – all stirred up herself because since April she'd been working at her first job, with Froggatt's Leather Goods to the British Commonwealth and Empire. Through July, August and for the rest of her life Nancy would be labouring there, like Edwin and Mabel Proffit.

Just long enough, Nancy hesitated.

Foolish, she'd later tell her best friend Violet Glover, and whoever else would listen. She'd say it harshly, looking away and gritting her teeth as though scolding someone. For fifteen minutes, she let Widow Caddlestone rattle and scrape a cast-iron poker in the fireplace next door at number 12. Nancy took heed. Paid attention all right.

But only that.

For the show of it really. Though not a soul was watching. The *voice* after all, she began to realize, was in her head; the *banging on the fender* was Mrs Caddlestone next door signalling for help.

No good chasing ghosts on the wallpaper, Nancy. All those people rushing up Kendrick Road to the railway station in the dawn-dark. You know who's really coming at 5 a.m. No good making shadow-puppets by the light from the streetlamp: an old man with a flat nose – 'Ode monny mawkin! Ode monny mawkin!' – the eagle in flight, the witch with a humpback and a chattering chin. You know it won't be Uncle Albert at the door. Foster parents are forever playing tricks. You know that, Nancy. Angels and fiends. It'll be those two ladies from the Home come to your door instead. Remember their names, Nancy? The orphanage women? Of course you do.

When the clanking stopped, Nancy touched her temple to the brickwork at the back of the hearth, sniffing at burnt newspaper and firewood, her ear jammed against a black cheek.

Nothing.

Who are we waiting for? thought Nancy, feeling a sneeze coming on.

Anyone waiting at all? For what?

Here it was, the Midlands Industrial Fortnight: so much, so much to cram in according to her foster mother, the entire Black Country turned inside out today and onto British Rail's Seaside Specials to Colwyn Bay, Rhyl, Llandudno.

Nancy Smith and Mrs Caddlestone with their heads in adjacent fireplaces as the whole world ran away.

How ridiculous.

Surely no one was waiting for answers.

Not today.

Walsall station had unlocked its gates early. First train to Blackpool at 5:30, Bath, Poole, Bournemouth 7:55, London half an hour later. 'Winston Churchill knows all about it,' Nancy's foster mother liked to say in her keeping-order tone of voice. '*And* our new Queen, Elizabeth,' as though the Establishment itself had given permission and would keep a respectful distance when sandbucket-waving trains came puffing through. Especially if Widow Caddlestone were in one of them; you don't mess with a working stiff's fourteen days.

Mabel Proffit – still tasting her fortieth birthday – would stay awake for nights at a time worried sick about the prospect of a holiday. As far as Nancy could see, Mabel's Industrial Fortnight was punishment beyond mortal ken, Genesis or no Genesis, a curse of the Kidsgrove boggart or Dick the Devil, and you would *pay*. Somehow it was all very, very wrong. You should never ever gad about like they do down south and in those shiny magazines.

Nancy, brushing soot from her tangly hair and full breasts, scoffed at her foster mother's bellyaching, then stumbled over the firedogs. Clapped her hands – one, two – and felt like that spirit in the Black Mere of Morridge just off the Buxton Road. Another story her *real* mother liked to tell – of the ravishing mermaid who'd lure travellers into the dark lakewater never to be seen again. Bet you Mabel doesn't know a sausage about that, thought Nancy. Ignoramus. No stories from Mabel Proffit to lighten a day stitching leather at Froggatt's.

But listen....

Remember those two ladies from the Home, Nancy? Mrs Thurston and Mrs Danks. Of course you do. That's a girl. The Birchills House ladies who taught you something and brought you here at seven years old? To number 10 Kendrick Road. To Mabel and Edwin Proffit who would give you all you needed instead of old wives' tales and potions from a fruitcake child-mum in the Rushall Road asylum. But you've wronged your foster parents, Nancy. Thankless guest in their terraced house, gremlin and snot. Mabel and Edwin are getting you back. There's no Nancy-sitter, an Uncle Albert Mallinder coming, only Revenge in sensible shoes. You know it. Stop pretending you don't.

The young teenager fancied she could still hear something. Widow Caddlestone or not. But then, since Nancy had left school and started working, she was always hearing something from the walls, windows and doors, maybe her mother in the asylum, even, or her father wherever – whatever – he was. Like someone reading the Lord's Prayer backward all the time, or shouting directions in Latin from inside a bowl of porridge.

She named this talking 'Summat Else.' It was like a doll or effigy she'd have to play with, the lips of a shell forced against her face. Are you listening?

'Mardy bugger,' Nancy said to the grate, wagging her finger at it, then at herself, and then at Mabel Proffit who hurried about upstairs in the bedroom getting Edwin, her husband, all dolled up for hell-on-sea wondering where on earth the downstairs racket was coming from. And finally – wag, waggle – at Old Misery Chatterbox next door beyond the damper and the jaundiced spinney wallpaper.

Nancy resumed the folding of her foster parents' Blackpool clothes – caggy-handedly now, and she knew why – into Edwin's scuffed leather suitcase that she'd perched on the arms of his favourite chair. She pretended not to notice the sooty fingerprints she was leaving on Mabel's brand-new nylon blouse from Carlton Fabrics and on Edwin's two Sunday shirts, but that wasn't why her entire body now began to goosepimple. 'Mardy bugger,' she said out loud again but more breathlessly. Look! Her fingers were shaking. She felt hot – and cold. 'I'll be me mother's ruin.' Suddenly, convulsing, she vomited into the neatly pressed clothes in her hands. Colman's-mustard-coloured sick.

Pig.

Rubbing at her lips in a panic.

'Oh 'eck. Now I'm a goner.'

But Nancy didn't for a moment believe it.

'Get the door will you, Nancy!' shouted Mabel from upstairs. 'How many times do I have to tell you?'

'Missus! Missus!' someone calling from outside.

A young voice. Male. Rat-a-tat-tat, on the pane.

In fact Nancy was sure by now that the rather dumpling-bodied Widow Caddlestone, on the other side of the hearth, would be stretched out – flat plonk – beside her always-Zebra-black-leaded-inglenook, maybe the poker still clenched in her puffy fingers with the wedding ring she could never twist off, and as dead as Doomsday with its tongue hanging out.

'Edwin can get it,' Nancy shouted back.

Poor Widow Caddlestone. Out for the count at sixty-five. No one heard your alarm. Except me.

'Anyone 'ome, missus?' shouted this adolescent at the door. Clatter, bang. Right old state. Letterbox dancing like a fiddler's elbow.

'Will you answer it, girl, before I box them ears o'yours?' yelled Edwin from somewhere else upstairs.

Nancy peeped through the letterbox.

Eye, eye.

It was Peter.

Sexy Peter Threnody with the stammer and bum-fluff lip.

Someone slapped her head.

Edwin.

'Ouch!'

At her side. Bushy eyebrows.

'What is it lad?' he said, yanking open the door. 'We've no time today.'

Fingernails. Edwin. Knocking her backwards into the banister.

Doe-faced Peter Threnody. How Nancy wanted to kiss him again.

Right now.

'I called the ambulance. But she's not breathing.'

Peter always fretting, pacing, delivering milk of a Saturday, for ninepence. Not many customers today.

Shelf-bracket grin.

'Who, lad?'

'Mrs Caddlestone, next door.'

Mabel Proffit appeared on the landing, her fashionable polkadot sun-dress in the light of a bulb – 'Oh!' in a squeak – and put her hand to her mouth.

'Thrown a seven she 'as, Mrs Proffit!'

Peter's pink dimples. Peter warm from running to the phone booth on the corner. Pointing next door.

'How did you get in, lad?' said Edwin rushing onto the street, his best shirttail flapping.

'Door's wide open,' said Peter.

Peter Gorgeous Threnody who wants to work in the ambulances when he's eighteen, ginger hair stuffed in his cap.

Peter, Peter.

'You what?' Edwin cried out. 'Blimey, it's a murder, lad.'

'No, Edwin. No. She never locks it,' chided Mabel.

'Isn't *that* the truth!' said Nancy, smirking for Peter.

Mabel Proffit gripped her handbag, the newel post, and a raincoat, like babes. '*You* wash your mouth out,' she said. The stairs complained noisily as polkadots made their way down.

'I will not.'

Let's watch the seaside trip unfold, thought Nancy. Just as Mabel Proffit likes holidays to be, ain't it? Two-week crucifixions with smutty postcards, rock and candy floss stuck in your teeth.

'Mrs Caddlestone's done you no harm, Nancy.'

'Did.'

'Beg pardon?'

'Did, did.'

And I – thought Nancy – like the roly-poly old darling next door, if she resurrects, will keep the home fires burning right through summer. Out of sight, out of mind. No fleeing the dead Widow Rattletrap for an apprentice like me.

A figure appeared in the doorway, startling Peter out of his wits.

'Albert Mallinder!' gasped Mabel, rushing the final steps into the hallway. 'You'll never believe it.'

Uncle Albert Mallinder, ever inspired by the Lord! As though he'd missed the Second Coming by a hair. Untipped cigarette hanging, with divinity, from his calloused fingers. The sweet odour of last evening's Black Satin stout filling the air.

Right on time for the clock-in, thought Nancy but with relief. Albert Mallinder looking like a funeral candlestick – as he did every day at Froggatt's – dressed head to toe in frail-looking black serge, with two Co-op carrier bags in hand, a Bible and roll of Blue Bird toffees sticking out of the one.

Just so we'd get him right.

Buttoned-down collar. Very thing for July.

'Have you been walkin' all night, Albert?' said Nancy.

'I have,' he replied. 'With our Saviour.'

Peter looked nervously over his shoulder.

'Partial to His nightcap too then, is He?' said Nancy, winking for Peter's benefit.

'Oh dear, Albert,' said Mabel.

'There's been a death,' said Edwin, looking pale. Peter Threnody swaying about behind him on the front step. 'Old lady next door.'

'I *knew* I heard something,' said Mabel, clutching her raincoat more tightly. 'I just knew.'

'It's no laughing matter, our Nancy,' said Edwin, swiping at the girl's head.

'I'm not!' she cried out, backing away towards the sitting-room.

'The widow?' enquired Albert Mallinder.

Peter seemed desperate for something more to happen. He gazed at the open door.

'Elderly,' opined Uncle Albert, with a sniff.

Nancy reappeared carrying Edwin's suitcase, summer cardigan and jacket.

'The 5:30 to Blackpool?' intoned Albert, as though offering communion but with the burden of wafers.

'Oh, we can't,' replied Mabel.

'Yes, you can,' said Nancy.

'But there's been a death,' Edwin explained, not for the first time. Hands in new pockets, he seemed more confounded than his forty-five years would allow.

'You'll lose your deposit,' Albert Mallinder reminded them gravely, as though speaking of Inferno. 'You've both worked so hard. *Seven pounds ten.*'

For an instant they all stood motionless on the brown-and-red checkered linoleum.

Seven pounds ten.

'Are you travellin' like that, then, love?' said Edwin.

'Like what?' Mabel demanded.

'With *them*.'

He indicated the polkadots.

'I've got me coat,' said Mabel, looking about her. 'Whatever you want, Edwin.'

Albert raised his head. '"Women shall not have authority over men; they must keep quiet." First book of Timothy, chapter two, verse twelve.'

'Exactly,' muttered Edwin, looking uneasy.

Nancy snorted.

'Better go, then,' said Edwin, raising his eyes to the heavens. 'Lights off upstairs, are they, love?'

'Blackout *on*,' said young Nancy.

'How do I look, then, dear?' said Edwin to his wife.

'Right lommock,' said Mabel, staring concernedly at Albert's head, still raised.

'Do ah?'

'Are you goin' to the seaside or not?' said Nancy, shaking the door handle.

'With a spotty wife? Gawd love us!'

'No lip for your Uncle Albert,' said Mabel. 'Be a good child, while he looks after you.'

Albert moved aside to let them pass.

Nancy rolled her eyes as the grief-stricken – Mabel's arm in his – took to the street before word got out on Kendrick Road.

'God speed,' said Albert.

'Cup o' tea, Peter?' said Nancy, more cheerfully than she'd really intended.

He shuffled about even more, bursting with something to say.

'Don't mind if *I* do,' said Albert, also looking very pained. '"We needs must die, and are as water spilt upon the ground which cannot be gathered up again".'

'Amen,' said Peter, grimacing.

'Second book of Samuel, chapter fourteen, verse fourteen,' Albert announced.

'Get the layer-out to come round,' said Peter, looking as though he might gallop at any second.

'Love a duck!' said Albert, touching the doorframe, his nicotine breath finally reaching Nancy. Christ, does Uncle stink. 'It's a few *miles!*'

'Nah. Only up Market Street, she is,' said Peter, twisting about. Whatever was wrong? 'Did me grandad up a treat the other week.'

'Once it's daylight we'll go, lad.'

'We'll need Holy Joe from the Baptists, as well,' Peter muttered. 'On Pritchett Road.'

'Heathen.'

'I know, I know,' said Nancy, waving them both indoors.

'I was wonderin'?' began Peter, his lip curling awkwardly.

'Toilet's out back, love,' replied Nancy, finally catching on.

Peter dashed inside.

'Lift the lid up!' Albert Mallinder growled after him, aiming the cigarette nub like a dart at the boy's back. With creaking boots, he dodged past Nancy and headed straight for the kitchen; his sombre, open jacket and carrier bags filling the hallway like a praying mantis, an odour of mothballs in his wake.

'Welcome,' said Nancy, taking a long look – then another – up the lamplit street and down. Go on then, the lot o' you, trains, coaches an' all. Skeddaddle, she thought, oddly defeated, before I nail yower trembling arses to the rails. She slammed the door like she'd won the pools, but lost the entry-coupon.

Get lost.

Coast was clear once more, letterbox clapped shut.

But no.

It was not enough for Nancy. Nothing was ever enough.

She lifted the net curtain at the front parlour window and let her nose flatten against the pane. Worse than chain-smoker breath and ash, the smell. At once it was the grimy face of this glorious July morning – Genesis, as Mabel called it. Day the world began on Kendrick Road – like piss-stench sighing in a wallpaper's leaf. 'Blackpool,' she whispered, not without awe, her lips pressed into the glass. 'Summat else to you and me.'

LET US EAT AND DRINK

Walsall, England. 1954

Froggatt's factory girls were livelier than usual, Bank Holiday week-end – no work till Tuesday!

Farther down the room, no-chin Albert Mallinder, with little stomach for rest by anyone else's decree save God's, was hunched over the bench. His devotion a trait grudgingly respected, his face a mulligrubs of the animal hide he stretched and turned day in, day out.

There he was – no hymns in his soul today. No Workers Playtime on the Home Service either. Just Albert Mallinder finishing off the slant of some complicated handstitching on a special-order harness gripped firmly in wooden clams. Hoping God wouldn't spy him, a Seventh-Day Adventist labouring on a Sabbath Saturday.

You couldn't help but admire mettle.

'Gather,' said a tired, throaty voice, unaccustomed – save on Saturdays at noon – to raising itself beyond an office manager's sober directives.

Bald, furrowed Mr Woods, keeper of Froggatt's Leather accounts, always backed away slightly from the coarser women who joked and flirted in the queue leading to his hatch at the end of the workfloor. Unlike these newest of the company employees who were *obliged* to work the Industrial Fortnight, in order to make ends meet he was forgoing a summer holiday himself – usually at Weston-super-Mare.

Most knew he was a father of five sickly young children and that his wife was 'wumman-licking him to an early grave'. This made the leather-stitching girls all the more brazen. A decent man who needed every bit of jollying.

'I'm off dancin' on me own tonight at the Mayfair, Mr Woods. 'Ow about comin' wi' me?' said Hazel Hunt, a wide-girthed machinist, leaning forward at the head of the line. 'Only a few shillings an' a cuddle, darlin'.'

Mr Woods grinned courageously as he handed over a week's pay. Hazel flapping the tiny manila envelope in the air. 'Oh, look! He's brought some johnnies, too!'

Screeches of laughter.

Hazel spun around on her fleshy ankles, winking at Violet Glover – Nancy's best friend – who herself was sparkling with mischief.

'Full o' moonshine and cures, yower natural mum – God bless 'er – and not only when she was older,' Albert Mallinder told Nancy the following Sunday morning as the Walsall city bus appeared. 'Don't know where she got 'em all from; must've bin from her own mother – she were a dark horse as well. We went to the same school, you know, yower mum Hannah and me. Did you know that? Canal Street Junior and Infants? I was three years above her. Did those foster parents of yours tell you that, I wonder – Mabel and Edwin Proffit?'

Albert stepped up into the bus. Nancy shook her head. 'I don't want to know,' she said.

'Well, y'going to hear it Nancy, 'cos it's yower birth mother we're talking about. Hannah – yower own flesh and blood.'

Nancy found a seat next to some churchy-looking women, hoping this would shut Albert up.

'Hannah's only twenty-eight now, Nancy. She may be a nutcase but her whole life's ahead of her.'

Nancy was exhausted. She'd not slept a wink after last night's Bank Holiday trek into Birmingham. Wildest night of her life.

'So is mine,' she muttered, looking out of the window.

'It's where you came from and it's not right everyone keeps it back from you.' 'They don't keep it from me, Uncle Albert. I don't want to know any more.' 'Just look at how y'turnin' out. Self-indulgence. It's painted all over you. Soul-defiling vice.' 'What vice? I went out with Violet Glover, that's all. Nothing happened.' 'Ah've got a ten-minute bus ride before we get to Rushall Road Asylum. That's time enough.'

'This is all about you, Albert Mallinder. I swear,' said Nancy, wishing upon wish the day would end. 'You and your dead wife Sally. You and that real mum of mine in Rushall loony bin. It's not about me. None of 'em's going to come back and be like they were. No matter how much you talk about 'em. They're all goners, Albert.'

At the leather factory and at home, Nancy was growing impatient with Albert Mallinder, her overseer. The conscientious, methodical man who now monitored her noon and night, at number 10 Kendrick Road as well as at Froggatt's, in place of Mabel and Edwin Proffit who were soaking up the cumulus in Blackpool. 'Fortnight in the Garden of Eden,' as her foster father always put it, chafing.

Bogeymen, bogeymen, everywhere.

Violet Glover – undoing her canvas apron – jostled Nancy from a daydream. 'So where's your glad rags?' she said softly, ruffling-out her bleached hair.

Nancy was too agitated to reply. She nodded toward a packing case underneath the preparing-and-cutting table in the centre of Froggatt's airless workroom.

Violet winked, locked her arm with Nancy's and stood on her toes.

'Come along there, Mr Woods!' she yelled above the two women in front. 'We know yower fond of a good cant over the garden fence, but really …'

More giggles and tut-tutting.

'Ower Nancy Smith 'ere's got 'alf the Reserve Army waiting outside. Ain't y', love?'

Violet planted a noisy smacker of a kiss to the back of her own hand which, again, brought colour to Mr Woods's face as well as to Nancy's.

On Saturday nights, from 7 p.m. until 11, most of Froggatt's youngest employees – those not gathered at the Jukebox Café on Wisemore and not chasing Teddy boys in their drainpipe trousers and brothel-creepers – would be quickstepping at the Mayfair or the Walsall Town Hall under Hedley Ward's Number One Broadcasting Orchestra.

This Saturday, though, was Hedley's Grand Holiday Dance, a pricey three shillings and sixpence. The crowd would be huge, servicemen getting in for a shilling less.

Ninety leather-stitching girls had talked of nothing else all week.

But Violet and Nancy held a trump card more winning than a mere Hedley Ward dance.

Escaping Walsall altogether, the two were bound for Birmingham, Nancy's first trip to England's Second City. Nearly a million people lived there. After her first ride in a train, she'd see her first ever live show, *South Pacific*, a musical at Brum's Theatre Royal. Nancy might as well have been going to the moon – a solution to everything.

'Where's your Uncle Albert, then?' said Violet, staring across Froggatt's workroom.

'At the board, wouldn't you know,' replied Nancy, fastening her charm bracelet. 'I'll catch him before I get dolled up.'

The girls at Froggatt's didn't call Albert Mallinder 'Rock of Gibraltar' for nothing. To Nancy, her newly arrived minder at Kendrick Road was more like a mile-long canal barge than a rock. A few rope-tugs of deception from the towpath and the man was set up for days. Or rather, for Saturday night – 'Genesis time' Nancy thought she'd call it, learning from foster mother Mabel – when her *own* world would begin.

As far as Albert Mallinder was concerned, Nancy and Violet would be spending Saturday afternoon together before an evening of dance at Walsall Town Hall. Simple as that. Albert Mallinder – like Mabel and Edwin Proffit – knew what he was told.

'But how can that be, Nancy?' At Froggatt's stitching board, the man was removing leather hockles protecting his fingers. 'Yower mother said y'wages were one pound, seventeen and six in yower pocket; and that you give the household – Mabel, that is – all but five shillings for y'keep.'

'So it is, Uncle Albert. But what with me being home sick a day last week ... twice. Then breaking that new Singer machine over there.'

'They stopped you some money then?'

'Fifteen shillings, Uncle.'

'Fifteen shillings!'

Albert Mallinder stared at his harness, and the hockles upon it.

Nancy looked out of the factory gates towards Walsall railway station.

'Oh, Nancy. Whatever next,' exclaimed Albert.

'With me being out for tea tonight and Sunday,' continued Nancy. 'Then out with Violet again on the Bank Holiday Monday. We'll need a lot less Elkes biscuits, for example, at Kendrick Road.'

'Well, I suppose.'

'I want to pay me fair share.'

'Oh, yes, dear. Of course, Nancy, whatever did you think ...?'

'If we're only two people now instead of the usual three, when it's Mum and Dad and me ...'

'We're two now.'

Nancy nodded, waiting for a sink to drain.

'Right, Uncle Albert. *We need less food.*'

'If you say so, Nancy. I don't know what Mabel and Edwin will think.'

I do.

Albert raised his head. Nancy sensed biblical chapters slithering up his gullet.

Quick!

'Look, Uncle,' said Nancy. 'How about I give you a full pound? That leaves a few shillings to get me through the week. I want to write a letter to Mum and Dad in Blackpool. Notepaper and stamps. New plants for the house.'

'One pound, Nancy?'

'I'll manage on my two shillings and sixpence, Uncle.'

Albert seemed too confused to do anything but accept the coins. 'You're eating tea with Violet?' he said, as though reassuring himself.

'Tonight I am, Uncle Albert. But I'll be home right after the dance. I've got me key.'

'Well, I'll wait up, love,' said Albert, most solemnly, resuming work on the special-order harness.

'Be seeing you, then.'

He'll be three sheets to the wind on Black Satin, Nancy knew that. Let him wait up. Snoring in Edwin Proffit's armchair by eight o'clock.

With that, she scooped her Boots plastic bag from the case beneath the cutting-table and hurried to the women's lavatory to put on her outfit.

'I'm sorry, Nancy. But that's what happened.' 'Like hell. You're havin' a right old time of it, ain't you, Albert?' 'I am not.' 'Then shut up. You can't just go on telling my story like this. How do I know if it's the right one?' 'It is, Nancy.' 'How do I know that? Eh?' 'Trust me.' 'Like writin' Mabel and Edwin that I'm out at all hours while they're on holiday in Blackpool?' 'I was angry, Nancy. You were seeing a man, I was sure.' 'There's no trustin' you, Albert Mallinder. You're a bad bloke.' 'God bless this child.' 'You've been makin' up stories all week, Uncle Albert. It's too much. I don't know what to believe.' 'All of it, Nancy. I'm telling you all of it.'

They sat on a bench at the entrance to Rushall Asylum.

'Are we going in then, Albert? It's why we've come.'

'Let me finish, love. Keep yower hands off me when I'm tellin' you the truth.'

'I'm sorry. Sorry I hit you.'

'Ungrateful hussy. You listen to me.'

Nancy crossed her legs defiantly and watched the Sunday traffic. I can't even strangle him quiet.

'Hannah was a good yarn, but she'd never have matched what was said about her. All of it wrong. All of it nastiness and superstition, Nancy. Satan himself had done it. That's what they all thought. What a laff. But just the rumour was enough, luv. Hannah had to go into hidin', with her stepfather in Ironbridge.

'But even there, people found out, crossed the street. Kids threw stones. Spat. Terrible things. The Smiths had always been under strain. Poor, they were. Weren't we all, then? But dirt-poor always – and everyone shunnin' them. They were never the same.

'Still, who should come into the world nine months later – March 1939 – but you, Nancy, dear?'

In Froggatt's loo, Violet Glover was applying a generous smearing of make-up to her gaunt features.

'Well, *I'm* going to hell in a blaze of glory,' said Nancy, undressing at a kick. 'I'm *rolling in dough!*'

'It's wha' y'can gerraway with,' said Violet, her philosophy for everything. 'Do I look like Marilyn Monroe yet?'

'Once we're out of here you will,' replied Nancy, humming a few bars of 'Some Enchanted Evening'. 'The lav doors don't set you off right.'

'Hardworking, Hannah yower mum, oh yes.' Albert went on, ' "In the sweat of thy face shalt thou eat bread." ' 'Deuteronomy, Uncle Albert?' 'Genesis, luv.' 'Three, verse six?' 'Are you makin' fun, Nancy?' 'You've used it before, Uncle.' Albert bowed his head. 'Took in laundry did Hannah, and found a cleanin' job with Mr and Mrs Cotterell, the horse-furniture family in them parts. Her folks sent a few pennies every now and again like, but not often. I hate to say it, but they did turn their backs on yower mum, even though it broke their hearts. Maybe Hannah was the final trouble they couldn't cope with, I don't know. People didn't know much in them days.

'Even when you both moved to Coalbrookdale – you and Hannah – she just about managed to keep you both going before comin' back to Walsall and the job at Sharpe's the locksmiths. But it were too much for a young girl. Too much. She managed alone for seven years, till she were twenty. No man would have her. In marriage. It were one thing after another.

'Trouble with her dad. He'd been on the beer again, but had gone back to the factory after a week of it; 'course, he was a zombie for days. But the bosses were pretty good to him. Sometimes I think they expected it. Certain men end up on benders. The life, Nancy. What else can some men do? Cruel. These lives are cruel on a man, Nancy. "Oh! My soul is among lions," Psalm fifty-seven, verse four. But yower granddaddy was okay for a month or so. Then one day, his wife Bertha noticed all these flared-up pimples on his arms and his back – and he'd had a cold for weeks. Dr Rawlings at the works said it were anthrax. It were. Dead before you could say boo to a blind horse.

'A few weeks later, some neighbour found young Hannah babbling at you, all cramped up – there was mess all over you both. Looked like you and Hannah hadn't washed for days. What on earth had you been eatin'? You were very, very sick, Nancy. Starving. They called in the police, my child. Poor Hannah. There was an inquiry. She'd had some kind of belt that was holdin' you to her chair. Maybe she'd just fallen asleep mindin' you. I know she didn't mean any harm. She just couldn't do it any more.

'They tried to get you in at the Open-Air School at Reedswood Park – for yower asthma. But in the end, it were the Birchills House orphanage that took you in, 'cos it were the only Home with places: Mrs Thurston and Mrs Danks. People speak very highly of their ways.'

'Uncle Albert,' Nancy groaned. 'Have you quite finished?'

'Didn't Albert Blue Balls twig about your pay?'

'Him?' said Nancy, carefully unrolling a pair of Mabel Proffit's best Nimbus nylons. 'He'd not see a canal bridge if it hit him in the dentures. Been dead a long time, that one.'

'Nancy.'

'Like all the other gnomes in this place,' she added, smoothing the stockings.

'Got all fifteen shillings to spend?'

'And more.'

'You witch!' said Violet, turning from the mirror for a second.

'Fogy workhorse, Albert is.'

'Don't take it too far, love.'

'He is so … And don't say it, Violet.'

'Say what?'

' "It's wha' y'can gerraway with." '

'Well, it is, isn't it?'

'Not always, Vi.'

'Albert Blue Balls' gotta keep his head above water, too, you know, Nancy.'

'What do you mean?'

'Albert Mallinder knows what you're up to, saying Froggatt's stopped you that fifteen shillings.'

'Why didn't he say, then?'

'Use yower loaf, love. You should see *his* place.'

'Eh?'

'Slum, Nance. Albert Mallinder's as poor as a rag-picker.'

'Get out.'

'You know the rest. Yower mum did try to look after you. But it were difficult once her folks decided they couldn't have you home, not after that. Even the kids turned their backs. Well, you know that. "Oh, they are a perverse generation, children in whom there is no faithfulness." ' 'Must be Deuteronomy,' said Nancy, trying to make out a billboard across the road. 'You can imagine how you'd have been treated, love – it's always been bad enough for them. People here don't forget these things. Blacksheep daughter, Nancy – the odd one out. What a joke! Now they'd found a way to keep you – and the war and all their silly heebie-jeebies – out of the way for good. Poor Hannah. Poor you, Nancy dear.'

'Are you hungry, Uncle Albert?'

'Hannah wanted to be Queen of Heaven citing chapter and verse until the end. That's what the nurses here told me, and that's what

Hannah's doin' up here on Rushall Road to this day, love. Talkin' to anythin' and anyone.'

'I know.'

'From Witches' Parliament to Earthly Paradise, Nancy. Creation of the Angels and the Fall of Lucifer, you never know where the blazes she is.'

'I know,' said Nancy. 'You'd fit right in there, yourself, Uncle Albert.'

'But she's happy, my child. You nearly died listening to her bloody stories, Nancy. That's the problem.'

'I've been listenin' to yours all week, Albert Mallinder. You're never like this at Froggatt's. But when the cat's away!'

'That's why you're so all over the map, Nancy. Yower natural mum Hannah's not connected up. Maybe a bit rubbed off on you, like. I don't mean that badly. You just need tekkin' in, like, from time to time, because you get . . . unravelled.

'White rabbits and black burrows, Hannah is. You do understand that, don't you? Blue elves in her eyes, day and night. Red toes. I'm so sorry, dear. But look how Mabel and Edwin have helped. Such a lovely couple. Everyone says. Quiet and steady, wouldn't you say? Always in their job. So don't you go makin' any big mistakes with men, you hear? You're much better off on Kendrick Road with the Proffits for a few more years yet.'

'Thanks for ravelling me up then, Uncle Albert. We can't sit on this bench all day. Do you want to go in or not?'

'Common as muck, that Albert. Council's gonna knock his whole street down,' said Violet Glover, putting the final touches to her lips.

'Fiddler's Court?'

'Yeah. Like they did wi' Temple Street last year.'

'I never.'

'He's on to a good thing with yower Mabel and Edwin.'

'Two weeks on Kendrick Road?'

'Even if it's with you, Nancy Smith.'

'Watch it.'

'Lost his old woman to the bottle and a dung pile of debt, he did.'

'No.'

'Oh ah. Sally Mallinder? Famous for it, she were. On the beer for weeks at a time. Every year it happened, then every few months.'

'Get out.'

'Pawned everything. Borrowed money. Nicked it. The lot.' Violet swirled around in her pink crepe dress.

'No wonder he's stuck to that workbench out there.'

'Then Sally kicked the bucket, all pickled and ready to go.'

'Saved a penny or two, that did.'

'Twenty-nine years old she was.'

'Pity.'

Nancy scowled. Too much make-up on her face.

'Your real dad was Phineas Ginder, by the way.'

'Oh, 'eck. More,' said Nancy, full of histories for a lifetime.

'The one who got hold of Hannah after the sun-wheels on Palfrey Hill. I'm sure of it. Phineas Ginder. Not Satan, for Christ's sake.'

'That's a relief then, ain't it?' said Nancy.

'Phineas was well known in Walsall. Young lad. Did odd jobs around the scrapyards, caretakin', haulin'. They'd asked him to be watchman for yower street. He were a one, I tell you. Cockfighter. Irish. So what d'you expect? Thickest Bogside accent you've ever heard. Then he started helpin' the layer-out, Mrs Badger – she were really getting on in years and she had the tremors from her drinking.

'Pity, 'cos when she got to move the corpses they was always jigglin' about so much it scared the bereaved. Then she was always forgettin' coins to put on the corpses' eyes and the cotton wool to stop all the leaks – started usin' anythin' that came to hand: loose buttons, bits of doily or a page out of the *Daily Mirror*. But Phineas kept her in business for the last few years before she pegged out herself.'

Nancy blew her nose. Surely he would run out of steam? This is what happens when a creep like Albert Mallinder gets a whiff of someone's past.

'Everyone with their wits about them suspected Phineas with your Hannah, though, no matter how godly his jobs got. But it couldn't be Satan AND Phineas Ginder who put you on this Earth, Nancy Smith. So, Black Country folk being folk, they went for Lucifer 'cos it were more entertainin' than some squint-eyed Paddy from a peat bog. Jesus, I don't know. Should have strung the bugger up if you ask me.

'But one or two local men had a word wi' our Phineas – and he disappeared. Everyone thought he'd enlisted. But I heard he'd joined the Stoke-on-Trent fire brigade. Second War began that year. 1939. Never saw hide nor hair of him again. "But oh, there is nothing covered, that shall not be revealed; and hid, that shall not be known."' He looked at Nancy. 'Know it dear? Matthew ten; twenty-six?'

But her eyes were too full to see.

'Funny, 'cos yer mummy's mum was born at the start of the FIRST war in 1914. Then you were born start of the SECOND, in '39. It makes the dates easy for you to remember when you reminisce, eh Nancy, love? War and War ... Don't cry now.... There, there.'

Nancy didn't know why she was crying. But she was. Maybe Uncle Albert would never stop talking.

She rubbed her eyes.

'Long line of wars – and rootless, hopeless men – you've come from, my girl. Child mums. Somethin' to tell your own kids once you're married.'

'Isn't it,' said Nancy.

'Maybe we should forget Hannah for today, eh Nance?'

'I was so looking forward to more tales, Uncle Albert.'

'What is there to say, really?'

Nancy began coughing uncontrollably. 'You've said more than Hannah ever could, Albert.'

'I suppose so, dear. "Let us eat and drink; for tomorrow we shall die."'

'The bus stop home is over there,' Nancy told him.

'I feel better now,' said Albert.

'That's what's important, Uncle. Can't bottle it up forever, can we?'

'Now you be a good girl, our Nancy. It's only another week before Mabel and Edwin come all the way home from Blackpool.'

'Right,' said Nancy, glancing at the Victorian building and its tended grounds. 'Have you ever heard of a place in Birmingham called "Little Canada", Uncle Albert?'

'Little Canada?'

'Somethin' I heard last night.'

'Of course I have, dear. Now what do you want to know?'

'Not a lot, Albert,' she replied. 'But here's a right story for you …'

'Poorhouse material after that, our Albert Mallinder,' explained Violet, as the two girls began arranging their handbags.

'That's one for the books, if ever I heard it,' said Nancy, sucking her cheeks in at the splintered mirror.

'From Mollesley's Dole at Fiddler's Court to Kendrick Road!' declared Violet.

'Albert Blue Balls has hit the jackpot at number 10 Kendrick? That's what yower sayin'?'

'That's it, sweetheart. Five-star livin'.'

As a last thought, Violet drew darker lines above Nancy's eyes.

'It's a dump, our house, Vi.'

'Not to him it's not.'

'So he's gonna keep the peace whatever I do?'

'Naturally. It's wha' he can gerraway with, right?'

Nancy stood back – and admired Violet's handiwork. 'Are y' 'avin' me on, Vi?'

'Cross me heart and hope to die.'

'What a fool I am!' said Nancy, twisting this way and that so her own dress would flare. 'I should've told him they'd stopped me a *quid.*'

NANCY'S BOY

Walsall, England. 1955

She had half an hour.

Tepid water, dab of coal-tar soap.

'You're a one,' she was saying, tickling his feet under the suds, making him giggle. 'Oh, you're a one.'

Nancy's final half hour.

On the radio, Bill Haley and the Comets were at a 'Rock Around the Clock'.

She emptied another jug into the stainless steel bowl. Kitchen window open, a fresh, spring breeze across the yard.

Sunshine in the bath.

'Eleven on the dot, Mr and Mrs Jones will be here,' said the retired nurse, supervisor of Walsall Adoption Society's Mother and Baby Home. 'I've paperwork.'

'Yes, Mrs Jerome,' replied Nancy, wearing a housecoat over her faded crimson skirt. She stood alongside baby Enoch, pouring water on the boy's shoulders. His legs kicking with glee.

'Keep the radio down, young madam,' she added, leaving the kitchen. 'Consider the other mothers as well as yourself.'

Nancy tickled Enoch under his arm until he squealed. Her hands helped his splash, the messiest mess.

'Oh, you're a sailor boy! Aren't you a sailor boy!'

Her face wet with Enoch's antics, Nancy lifted him into a towel and patted his body dry, carefully wiping the tiny fingers, his bottom, the backs of Enoch's knees, and inside his sticky-out ears.

Time of their lives.

Puddles on the kitchen floor. Nancy's hair more a tangle than usual, tied back with elastic.

'Five o'clock, six o'clock, seven o'clock rock, We're gonna rock around the clock tonight,' continued Haley and his Comets.

Nancy danced baby in the air. Enoch gurgled, arms and feet swimming.

Mrs Jerome had arranged with Nancy's new employer – Patterson and Stone leather manufacturers on Frederick Street, 'only a brisk half hour's walk across Walsall, dear' – for a morning off work: one or two hours at Paddock Lane readying Enoch and packing up her own clothes, an hour to find lodgings before the factory's afternoon shift at one o'clock.

When babies left Paddock Lane, so did the mothers. No exceptions. This was Nancy's final day as well. 'Locate a room in *this* area, Nancy; and near Patterson and Stone,' Mrs Jerome had instructed. 'We don't want you spitting distance from Kendrick Road where your foster parents are, or anywhere on that side of town, do we? Bumping into Edwin and Mabel Proffit, bless them.'

Nancy had lost any fear. She felt invincible. Who could stand in her way after these nine months? What frighten her?

Enoch played with his mother's fingers as she reached for the talcum powder and began dusting his buttocks.

Nancy's soul had closed like a fist on the voices that cascaded through her head and pounded at the door. In the months since Halloween, when her foster father Edwin Proffit had found her spewing in the ginnel next to the house on Kendrick, Nancy Smith had seen her world disappear like a permanent eclipse. Voices sounded – maybe Nancy even *heard*. But nothing remained for long. Not anymore. Why remember voices? One play of a turntable was rock enough.

Uncle Albert Mallinder – her caregiver during the Industrial Fortnight – had kept his trap closed when the Proffits returned from their Blackpool holiday. He had not taken sides with Nancy's foster parents until the end, and with them he thought it best the girl start over as an 'independent lass' seeing as she enjoyed it so much.

But Uncle Albert – the morning after Nancy's Birmingham-late-night-out episode – had hauled the child on a fruitless 'corrective' trip to Rushall Road Asylum to visit her 'real mum' Hannah. Not correction enough. He did Nancy, his temporary summer charge, the added favour of a much-resisted 'educational' outing to Walsall public library and an *Atlas of the World*. 'Open at page nine, child,' Uncle Albert had demanded. 'Chapter on British Commonwealth. See there? Those large pink puzzle pieces. Take a good, long look at Canada.'

Nancy had never studied a book so closely in her life, tongue curled, forefinger pursuing the major Canadian cities: Vancouver, Edmonton, Winnipeg, Montreal ... Toronto? How goading that place, even now! On Lake Ontario – towards the EAST of the country? That's not what Curtis, her Birmingham-late-night-out new friend – 'Canadian expatriate, that's me' – had said.

'With your left hand, can you find me British Columbia, Nancy? The Rocky Mountains? Pacific? That's it. Keep your finger on Vancouver, there's a dear.' To be co-operative, Nancy pressed harder into the page, face darkening. 'With your right hand, show me Toronto on that lake. That's a girl.' Nancy was a pair of calipers fully extended. 'He's from Toronto, British Columbia, this fella Curtis?'

What does a Canadian bloke do with his bollocks, standing so far apart like that, wondered Nancy? The lying bugger.

'"There is nothing covered, that shall not be revealed; and hid, that shall not be known. Especially where men are concerned." Matthew ten, verse twenty-six,' Uncle Albert had crowed, amending scripture to suit an occasion.

Nancy had fled the reading-room while Uncle Albert returned *the truth* (for once not a Bible) to its shelf. No wonder Curtis's Longbridge telephone number was not in service. Little Canada – as he called his area of immigrant Birmingham because it was so full of 'Canucks' – had never been hooked up for his ladies, or for anyone. Curtis and geography were as foul as his Black Country 'Aynuk and Ayli' jokes. Could you believe anything he had uttered? Likely he wasn't a Canadian expatriate at all. Simply a Brummie, Austin factory worker. With blarney. That's what they made in

Longbridge: engine parts, dreamers and tommyrot.

Nancy began looking upon Albert with new eyes. Yet it was too late. Uncle Albert needed to survive at Froggatt's where he and the Proffits worked and where Nancy, in November, had received her notice. He offered to procure Nancy an abortion. When she refused, down came the wrath of God. Uncle Bible-Thumper jumped on the Proffit bandwagon and – with humility – reminded everyone about ditches and fallen women.

A message that her best friend Violet Glover, in a rage at Nancy's 'duplicity', digested eagerly – and like the others, left Nancy to 'her better life. Don't ever use anywun like that again. You're appallin', Nancy Smith. I was tryin' to be yower pal that night, not some chaperone or a gooseberry. Yow went off down that canal wi' a complete – and pie-eyed – stranger. Anythin' could've happened.'

Violet had a right to feel betrayed. Nancy had deceived her on their first night out – ever – in the big metropolis of Birmingham. To see that grand *South Pacific*. Not *blokes*. Madcap idea, Nancy suggesting a pub afterwards. Violet was her closest ally – and Nancy had failed her. Gunning for a man – any one; the first who looked – and offering him her body. 'Yow are reckless, Nancy Smith. Don't care twopence about anywun but yowerself. Tek my advice and settle down. Yow could tek a leaf out o' Mabel and Edwin's book.' 'That's a laff,' Nancy told her, 'Edwin Proffit only married 'er 'cos she were the best seamer-stitcher on his line at Froggatt's. It meant 'e could get his work back faster.'

Violet, however, was not a patch on Peter Threnody who had believed that Nancy would eventually be *his* love. One evening after work, late November, the seventeen-year-old took pregnant Nancy for a stroll in Walsall Arboretum. He had heard the news, of course, and offered to marry her. Gentleman to the end. 'But only if you abort the kid, Nance. Me mother knows a woman....' When she declined, Peter decked her. He was always on the boil. Like the other Froggatt's employees, Peter stood up for children-from-wedlock, Jesus and heaven. Or for abortions first. Nancy was beginning to find men – foster parents and colleagues – daunting. There were days when isolated Paddock Lane and its nondescript shelter was like rock 'n' roll heaven, where pregnancy set the fallen free.

January 1955 at the Mother and Baby Home – snowiest thirty-day cold snap in history, according to the radio – and Nancy, in Sunday funk, had lain in a bathtub smoothing her swollen belly. 'Stay in, child,' she would whisper, perspiration glistening on her forehead. Eyebrows.

'Don't come out.'

Unvisited, miserable, and depleted after work at Patterson and Stone, most evenings she would flip through Mrs Jerome's magazines – *Life*, *Vogue* – and chat to the other teenaged girls who, like her, were in the factory until their eighth month. On an old settee, Nancy would often fall asleep over a cup of Horlicks and the biscuit – until Mrs Jerome could no longer take the 'idle young', and sent everyone to bed 'hands on top of bedspreads, please'.

'I'm going to give you away, little bodkin.'

One of these winter Sundays – after a particularly doleful soak – Nancy had considered a last and foreshortened walk along the part-frozen canal. There was a lock basin near Birchills House, her orphanage before being fostered out to the Proffits. You could fall through like a rabbit down its hole.

Nancy sat in her room, trying to read a copy of *The Sphere* from May the previous year, one of numerous used publications circulated by the Salvation Army or one of the Moral Welfare ladies who visited. It was mainly a collection of photographs about the homecoming of a new, young Queen Elizabeth II after her six-month tour of the British Commonwealth and Empire.

She and the Duke of Edinburgh had been around the world: Fiji and Tonga where the royals had witnessed paddle dancing and hula. New Zealand, Australia, Uganda to open the Owen Falls Dam, Aden, Malta, Gibraltar, Ceylon, Bermuda, Jamaica. It felt like reading the programme to last summer's *South Pacific*. Unpronounceable, unknown places.

Nancy studied every inch of the publication. Mother-to-be:

wide-eyed, exhausted. Even the advertisements were from another universe: Union Castle cruises to South Africa, Cunard, Home Lines' six days to Canada on the *S.S. Atlantic*, P&O to Lisbon and Casablanca. Ford Consul cars 'for the city man, the traveller, doctor, golfer....' English Electric modern kitchens, Booth's Dry Gin for 'loyal toasts the world over'.

Nancy left *The Sphere* open on the eiderdown and looked out at the snowbound lane. St. Matthew's spire in the distance, slate roofs. Dappled walls. Drainpipes. Net curtains. A window sill. Her bed and dresser. The Queen looked little older than she, it seemed to Nancy. The Royal Yacht *Britannia* had sailed up the Thames and moored at the Tower of London, crowds lining the bankside.

Thousands cheered in Trafalgar Square and the Mall, rejoicing all night. Rejoicing? Her Majesty was home. Why did everyone bother so much? No one in Walsall, save possibly Mabel Proffit, had known about this *return*, had they? The tour? Last year, I was at Froggatt's dreaming of a trip to Birmingham one day, she thought. No dukes or queens in Brum. Who knew about a *homecoming*?

Nancy closed the pages, slipping the magazine onto the linoleum floor. This was England. She did not live there. Nancy lived in Walsall, a nowhere place. Seeing these pictures, the girl smirked at her daft, romantic fantasies. She lived in the English Midlands. Industrial Black Country. You were happy about that. Or died a death before your time – a living death – just like Mabel and Edwin Proffit. No wonder so many revolutions and angry people started here. Oswald Mosley's fascist Blackshirts, for one. That was the lesson of Paddock Lane, wasn't it? Except for the baby. Enoch would have his freedom. 'Come out, I've changed my mind,' she told her belly-button. 'Come out, get out. England's in hiding. All clear, Enoch!'

The fetus grew. Nancy became accustomed to the baby's weight, the kicking. By March, after her sixteenth birthday, Nancy's feelings had evolved. More like a mother, she began to welcome the child. 'Yes, my sunshine?' she would say, lying in a bath of Epsom salts, feeling Enoch's body kick.

Mabel Proffit had always called the Walsall Industrial Fortnight

'Genesis. The day the world begins for the likes of us.' Maybe there was a grain of something in her foster mother's exaggeration, in a two-week factory holiday. It allowed Nancy to escape Uncle Albert for a night and, with Violet Glover, see her first musical. Nancy might have lost her virginity on a towpath – and met a Curtis, some Dick the Devil or Kidsgrove Braggart – but now there was Enoch.

'Show the sods, little one,' she whispered, thrusting her belly above the saline water to ease her aching back. 'Show 'em my spunk.'

Quarter to eleven. Bill Haley long gone.

It was so easy to make Enoch giggle. She rocked him in her arms, felt his nakedness against her bosom, sensed every layer of muscle, tendon and bone.

'Mr and Mrs Jones will do a better job than you,' Mrs Jerome had told her, three days after the boy was born, 'They're so determined to raise a child in a normal household. I knew you'd be pleased we can situate him.'

But Nancy was not.

She felt she would never again be happy about anything.

'Yow've always got me, Enoch,' she said, humming another tune on the radio. 'Got me running along those little arms and legs.' She spider-ran her fingers over his tummy. 'And ah'm the juice in them tiggly-wiggly toes, wee-wee-wee-wee-wee,' she squeaked like a piglet. 'We're going to dress yow up now, little Enoch,' she told him. 'Make y' a Prince for Mr and Mrs Jones. Aren't yow the lucky boy? They're goin' to love y' to death. Just watch.'

Nancy was bitter about Curtis, if that was his real name, but the hurt feelings subsided with this coming of spring; just like Edwin Proffit's hostility to another holiday fortnight at Cliffview Terrace, Blackpool. But not because of crocuses, chocolate bunnies and daffodils. But *Schadenfreude* – what bounty Curtis was going to miss. She relished misfortune for a trickster. Curtis 'from Toronto, British Columbia' would never know his natural child, the real ending to their canal-side love. Maybe Curtis would prefer it that way.

Shamefully, she still desired him. One last time, she could take him, even if Toronto were on the moon.

Nancy would always visit Birmingham – the theatre, Needless Alley and that Wheatsheaf Arms where 'Genesis' really got off the ground. Wardrobe or no wardrobe, she could make that trip again. Violet Glover or not. Curtis. If Nancy Smith was going to stay put in Walsall, she was going to *soar*.

One day, she would soar.

'Who's the father?' Edwin Proffit had yelled, in the front room, last Halloween as local kids ran by in ghoulish costumes – and her foster father covered his eyes. 'Just don't tell me it's a Paki or some other ruddy tarbrush.' Edwin had kicked Nancy into the house from the ginnel where he'd found her vomiting. 'How many men 'as she 'ad?' he said to Mabel as though his wife were privy to all.

'The one,' said his wife, for safety's sake half concealed by the nearest furniture.

'It were a terrible mistake, Dad.'

'She's very sorry, Edwin,' added Mabel.

'I am sorry, Dad,' Nancy repeated, splashes of sick across her Froggatt's work shoes.

'Is he your fella, then? Who is he, girl?'

Nancy looked at her boots. Mabel shook her head.

'Only a decent man would admit to anythin',' he carried on. 'But one thing's for certain,' said Edwin, grimly. 'You're out of here next week, young lady. No ifs or buts.'

'What do you mean, Edwin?' asked Mabel, hand to her mouth.

'No tart's livin' under ma roof, Mabel. When I said I'd be a father, I meant to one bebby, not two.'

'Edwin, no. We can't,' his wife replied, her voice near choking. 'Where would she go?'

'Shoulda thought o' that before droppin' her knickers.'

'Edwin!'

'Send her back to Birchills House. They knock sense into trollops.'

'No, Dad, please.' Nancy, too weak. 'I promise I won't do it again, ever.'

'Back to where yow cum from!' he thundered.

'No, Edwin. We'll not do that,' insisted Mabel. For no apparent reason, she snatched at the lace doily gracing her best-china cabinet.

'We'll do what ah say,' he stated, raising his bare hand to them. 'Girl's out o' here, come Monday mornin', for good. You're gonna get Mrs Danks and Mrs Thurston round to tek 'er. Got it?'

'Over my dead body,' Mabel replied, now lowering her voice as more children passed the window. 'Never, Edwin. There's the Adoption Society, for heaven's sake. She's not evil. An orphanage is no place for her now. You can be so hateful.'

'I never want to see that whore again,' he snapped back, reaching for his coat and scarf. 'Get out o' mah way, the two o' ye.'

Nancy laid Enoch on the table to powder his abdomen and wrap the nappy, fastening it securely with a king-size safety pin. Mrs Jerome had found some second-hand lime-green woollen booties at the market along with a crocheted jacket in lighter shade, to go on top of Enoch's singlet. Carefully, Nancy tucked him into these new clothes, glancing at his eyes.

Had he suspected? She felt her guilt so deeply. Motherly smile a fraud.

'What will y'ever think of me, Enoch?' she said as brightly as she could. 'Letting y'go to lovely Mr and Mrs Jones like this? But yow'll be such a bonny lad.'

She undid the blue housecoat and slipped a breast from beneath its cup, lifting Enoch gently to her nipple. 'One for mummy, Enoch?' With milk, he'll be asleep when they arrive. She could not bear the thought he might cry out for her. 'Drink, sweetheart. For your trip home.'

At 10:55, the kitchen door opened.

'Nancy's boy ready?' said Mrs Jerome, cheerfully.

Nancy touched her lip to quieten the woman.

Mrs Jerome noticed the feeding. 'Come along, dear,' she said, no more quietly. 'Bring him to my office and leave your housecoat by the sink.'

In November, the Adoption Society – in the unequivocal voice of Mrs Jerome – had made it a condition of Nancy's residency at Paddock Lane that she work a full-time job of their finding, turn over all her wages, and keep no company with the opposite sex. Only *family* might visit between 8 p.m. and 8:30.

In return, Nancy would be fed and housed until six weeks after the baby was born. The child, whether adopted or transferred to the area orphanage in Birchills, would be of no concern to Nancy after that date. As her legal guardians, the Proffits had signed the necessary documents. Nancy's foster parents also requested that their daughter be removed 'a respectable distance' to the Society's North Road Hostel in Wolverhampton just prior to the birth at New Cross Hospital, 'and for the immediate post-natal period'.

'You do understand, don't you, Nancy?' Mrs Jerome had said on the first morning, loaning her a handkerchief. 'No one's very pleased with you. Can you blame them? But we're here to help you get it all over and done with. Time for work now. We've found you a job at Patterson and Stone. Here are the directions. You can leave your suitcase in my office. Unpack it when you get back this evening. The gaffer is Mr Harold Sheldon. Second floor. He knows all about you. So, behave. Off you go now. Start's at seven. The Proffit family was unable to offer any financial assistance, Nancy. But work is good for a gal. Sign this before you leave. It confirms everything I've just said....'

'No, dear, you don't need a front-door key. I am always here and waiting for you.' 'If it's a girl I want it to be called Ellie May,' Nancy had announced, desperate to speak. 'Or if it's a boy, Enoch Joseph.' (According to Uncle Albert Mallinder, 'Enoch' meant long life.) 'Those rights are signed away.' 'I've signed nothing, Missus.' 'But Mr and Mrs Proffit have.' 'It's not their baby. I'm only asking one little thing. Please, Mrs Jerome.' 'It's not usual, dear.' 'Well there's always the cut, isn't there?' 'I beg your pardon?' 'The cut, Mrs Jerome. I'll

jump in the cut and drown us both, like monkey-man. Haunt the lot
o' yow.' 'Don't you threaten me, young madam. I'll see what I can do.
No promises. Sign.' 'No, Missus. Write down what I've asked at the
bottom there. Then I'll sign.' 'You've got some nerve, Nancy Smith.'
'Even if it's only the middle name, I want something of mine to go
with the baby.' '*Read*, Nancy,' said Mrs Jerome, inflamed. 'Thank
you, Missus. Have yow ever had a child of your own?'

'You've got some addresses from the *Walsall Observer* for lodgings,
haven't you?' said Mrs Jerome. 'Here's the Adoption Society's ten
shillings to start you off.'

'Yes, Missus.'

'Make sure you do take a room. No shilly-shallying or a pen-
north o' chips. Try to respect the position you're in, dear. And your
age. People are not going to welcome you with open arms. Or *save*
you.'

'No.'

'Good girl,' and she opened the office door. 'Isn't Enoch a beau-
tiful boy?' said Mrs Jerome, as though it were the first time. 'Put him
on the desk here by the blotter. Sign the release form, if you will.'

Nancy wrote her name.

Ignoring Mrs Jerome's instruction, she held Enoch at her waist.
The boy's eyes closing.

'There's a crib over there,' said Mrs Jerome, checking the con-
sent papers and indicating that Nancy should now leave. 'Mr and
Mrs Jones are waiting in the hall.'

Beyond that other door, next to the crib.

Nancy laid Enoch – sound asleep – on the pocket-pillow and
drew the coverlet over him. For a few seconds she looked at her son,
then bent down and kissed his forehead. 'I love you, Enoch Joseph
Smith,' she said quietly. 'Live long for me, little bodkin. Be strong.'

Mrs Jerome ushered Nancy towards the door that led to the
kitchen. 'Have yourself a glass of water before you go, child,' she
said. 'Be back at Patterson and Stone *pronto*. I gave them my word.'

Nancy opened one door, Mrs Jerome invited new parents by the other. Nancy hesitated, catching sight of Mrs Jones's coat. But shut the door abruptly, tears smearing her cheeks. 'Forgive me, Enoch.'

As Nancy made to hurry, a sharp tug ripped her skirt. For horrifying seconds, the girl imagined Enoch's hand. 'Oh, *please!*' she cried out, freeing herself by opening the door slightly – glimpsing the woman bent over the crib, arms reaching down. Mrs Jones shot a glance at the teenager clutching ribbon to her side.

Terror in the older woman's eye.

Nancy let the doorknob slip.

PART FOUR

LETTERS

The General Register Office (Adoptions Section)
Titchfield, Hants

E. Jones, Esq.
c/o Major Rupert Chubb
Sassoon Lodge, 33, Old Steine Road
Brighton, Sussex

February 12, 1974

Dear Mr Jones,

Your letter to St Catherine's House in London has been forwarded to me by a counsellor, Mrs Jessica Manley. I apologize for the delay in replying.

Unfortunately, our office is precluded under Section 20(5) of the Adoption Act 1958 from providing any person with information which would link an entry in the Adopted Children's Register and the corresponding entry in the Birth Register, except under an order of a court of competent jurisdiction.

In the future, however, were provision to be made and this become law it would be possible to release to an adopted person over the age of eighteen years information concerning his or her natural parents. I would therefore advise you to write again to this office should the provision be made.

Regards,

H. Pope (Mrs)

St. Catherine's House
10 Kingsway, London WC2B 6JP

E. Jones, Esq.
Sassoon Lodge, 33, Old Steine Road
Brighton, Sussex

15 May, 1974

Dear Mr Jones,

In February, I wrote concerning adoptees' access to original birth information. My colleague in Titchfield, Mrs Pope, furnished additional details. Since that time, the British government has reviewed adoption legislation. I am pleased to advise that the General Register Office has received notice that in autumn 1975 a Children's Act will become law. An Adoption Act is expected the year after that.

Historically, it was thought best for all concerned that an adopted person's break with the past should be final. Parents placing their offspring for adoption were told that the child would not have access to his/her original birth certificate. The forthcoming Acts reflect increased understanding of the adoptee's circumstances: that adoption may offer a child full membership in a new family – but that information about real origins may still be important.

Our department has already experienced considerable demand upon its resources as a result of these changes. If you were adopted before the forthcoming Children's Act in November 1975, you are required by law to see our social worker (called a counsellor) before you may obtain information from your original birth certificate.

In this regard, we have begun to set interviews that will take place from November 1975 onward. I invite you to contact our office.

Sincerely,

Jessica Manley

Mail Office – Classifieds
The *Walsall Observer*
96–98, The Bridge
Walsall, Staffordshire

E. Jones, Esq.
2, Calle Balsareny
Barcelona, 00897
Spain

December 1st, 1975

Dear Mr Jones,

We are in receipt of your notice and payment for a week's insertion in the 'Personal' column:

NANCY SMITH – Once resident of Paddock Lane, Walsall and of North Road, Wolverhampton (31st March, 1955 – New Cross Hospital) or anyone who knows of her. Please contact Mr Enoch Jones, 2, Calle Balsareny, Barcelona, 00897, Spain.

Thank you for choosing the *Walsall Observer*.

Yours faithfully,

Sandra Clunderson

12, Holtshill Lane
Walsall
Staffordshire
England

E. Jones, Esq.
2, Calle Balsareny
Barcelona, 00897
Spain

December 9th 1975

Dear Mr Jones,

With reference to your enquiry in the 'Personals' of the Walsall newspaper about Nancy Smith, I am a very close friend of Nancy's and at
her request I am writing to you to find out exactly what you would
like to know or what your intentions are.

As you can appreciate this has come as a shock to Nancy, so I
have agreed to act as a go-between should you wish to make further
contact.

Yours sincerely,

Mrs F. Bentley

Central England Post-Adoption Service
52, Caldmore Road, Walsall

Mrs Nancy Threnody, c/o Mrs Bentley
12, Holtshill Lane, Walsall
Staffordshire

January 15, 1976

Dear Mrs Threnody,

I hope you may be able to help us. My colleague Sylvia McTavish and I have been helping an Enoch, who now lives in Spain, to locate relatives he lost touch with many years ago. We have managed to establish that he is related to a Smith family from the Walsall area. We understand your maiden name was Smith and wondered if you may be able to assist us with our enquiry, which is of course made difficult by the considerable number of Smiths we need to consider.

I visited a Mrs Bentley this morning to substantiate that she is indeed your close friend. We have received some assistance in our work from her (enclosed is Mrs Bentley's recent letter to Enoch forwarded to our office). Any help you yourself could offer would be most appreciated. Enoch was born in Wolverhampton in the spring of 1955.

In the strictest confidence, we look forward to your telephone call.

Yours sincerely,

Polly Duckett

Central England Post-Adoption Service
52, Caldmore Road, Walsall, England

Enoch Jones
2, Calle Balsareny
Barcelona, 00897
Spain

January 30, 1976

Dear Mr Jones,

I regret that I have not had a telephone call from you in order to
properly negotiate a meeting with Nancy Threnody (formerly
Smith) who, I can now confirm, is indeed your birth mother and
have therefore had to make arrangements I would much prefer to
have discussed with you. Nevertheless I trust these will be acceptable, as Nancy would be most disturbed if this matter which has
been on her mind since December cannot be resolved quickly.

On Sunday February 29th at 5 p.m., Nancy will be at the Sandhill Arms Hotel (steakhouse and pub) which is at Stonnall off the
A461 between Walsall and Lichfield. Nancy's husband Peter advises
that once you have passed the A452 (Chester Road) you should see
the hotel on your right. If you reach Carter's Field Lane you have
gone too far.

It is a large establishment with children's facilities and well
known to Nancy and her family so she will feel comfortable there.
She will be at the opposite end to the family area near the entrance
from the car park – tables are set out in alcoves.

Peter will be bringing Nancy to the venue – she does not drive –
but I have suggested that you and she should have the time alone
together. If a friend drives you there perhaps he/she would likewise

'melt into the background' to begin with. It may well be advisable not to drive yourself and I imagine the Sandhill Arms is not easily reached by public transport. You may however decide to go alone by taxi – I'm sure any driver at either Walsall or Lichfield stations knows the place.

I met Nancy last Wednesday. She is a friendly, dark-haired lady of 37 and she told me about her family. A few brief details follow which may be a starting point for conversation.

She married Peter Threnody in September 1957 when she was eighteen. She works as a stitcher in a leather factory. Peter is an ambulance driver. They live in Walsall and have a son Mark (19) and a daughter Grace (16). Neither child is married – both still live at home. Enclosed is a photograph of Nancy. She does not possess any others but has lent me this to enable you to recognize her. Please return it to her, although I am sure she would be happy for you to have a copy. Also please remember that she has no means, other than her own imagination, of recognizing you.

This is obviously not how we would choose to provide an intermediary service but one which has been dictated to us by your placing of the newspaper advertisement (!) and your living in a foreign country. I trust you will be able to meet Nancy as set out above.

Sincerely,

Polly Duckett

Notes

Most of the stories in this collection were previously published, and subsequently revised. 'Now Showing' in *Pagitica* (2:4, 2004): 11–21, shortlisted for its International Literary Competition 2003. 'There's a Comma after Love' as 'Notfall' in the *Malahat Review* (Fall, 36:1, 1997): 26–36. 'Lessons in Space' in *Quarry* (44:2, 1996): 111–122; 'Heaven' in the U.S. anthology *Everything I Have Is Blue*; a section of it as 'Service' in Canada's Arsenal Pulp Press series *Quickies 3* (2003): 176–178. 'The Bombmaker' was published in Canada as 'Enoch Jones and the Bombmaker' in *Pagitica* (2:2, 2002): 60–75; in the U.S. with *Blithe House Quarterly* (Feature story/Summer, 6:3, 2002); was nominated for the U.S. *e2ink-2 Best of the Online Journals Anthology 2003*; became a finalist in America's New Century Writer Awards 2002; was shortlisted for Canada's *Prism international* Short Story Competition; and an excerpt appeared as 'Naked Night' in *Quickies 2* (Fall, 1999): 68–71. 'First Steps First' came out in the Banff Press anthology *Intersections* (Fall, 2000): 42–46. 'Travestís' in the U.S. online journal *Lodestar* (Summer, 2004). 'You Dress Up, You Dance' in the *Antigonish Review* (Fall, 2004). 'Once Upon a Prissy' in *Prism international* (Fall, 42:1, 2003): 64–72. 'Summat Else' appeared in the *Malahat Review* (Fall, 128, 1999): 76–84. 'Let Us Eat and Drink' was published in the *New Quarterly* (Special Issue/'Bad Men Who Love Jesus', Spring, 86, 2003): 122–137, and submitted by the *New Quarterly* for a National Magazine Award 2004 – Fiction Category.

Acknowledgements

I thank John Metcalf for taking me on, and for his argus-like, yet respectful, editorial suggestions; Jack Illingworth for a benevolent introduction to the Porcupine's Quill, Tim and Elke Inkster; literary consultant Bethany Gibson and the staff of Canada's literary journals for their encouragement. In American publications, I am indebted to editors Wendell Ricketts, Aaron Jason, Jarrett Walker and Aldo Alvarez. In Spain, the Omedes Regàs family, John Eastman, Lorna Dunn. The faculty and colleagues of Banff Writers Studio 1996, the Leighton Studios team and Banff Centre Press have always been disarmingly supportive and continue to be so. Colin Bernhardt. Friends and others, regardless: Idelmar Ramos, Cheryl Porter, Bernard Trossman, the late Pauline Heron, Cathy Thompson and Jim Weisz, Curtis Gillespie, Donna MacFarlane, Lee Easton, Michel Rice and Lavinia Inbar. I acknowledge generous support from the Canada Council for the Arts, Mohawk College, and the Ontario Arts Council.

British-born Royston Tester grew up in Birmingham. Before emigrating to Canada in 1978, he lived in Barcelona, London and Melbourne. A Canadian citizen, he is a fellow of the Hawthornden International Writers Retreat in Scotland, the Valparaíso Foundation in Spain and is a frequent Leighton Studio artist-resident at the Banff Centre for the Arts, Alberta. He was winner of the 1998 Chapters Short Fiction Prize and shortlisted for the 2000 Prism international Short Story Competition. Tester's work has appeared in numerous Canadian literary journals, including *Descant*, the *New Quarterly*, the *Antigonish Review* and the *Malahat Review*. Currently working on a second collection of stories, *You Turn Your Back* and a novel, *For the English to See*, he lives in Toronto's 'Little Italy'.